THE GEMINI RISING ROCKIN' MACHINE

FUCKAHOLIC
THE BOOK OF BAD SONGS

Featuring The Book: Fuckaholic

Also Featuring:

Most Have Been Renamed
But All Are Bad Songs Now

Untitled Sex Story #1

Untitled Sex Story #2

Blake and Barbara (John)
(Extended Website Version)

The First Four New Unnumbered
Mind Rockin' Songs

**Copyright 2018 by
The Gemini Rising Rockin' Machine**

**ISBN-13: 978-0-578-61792-3 (Gemini Rising
Rockin' Machine,The)**

ISBN-10: 0-578-61792-7

The characters and events described in this book are
fictional. Any resemblance between the characters and
any person including their names, living or dead, is
purely coincidental.

Because of the mature themes presented within, reader
discretion is advised.

WARNING:
Must be Eighteen or older to buy, read or sing along to
this Mind Rockin' book.

For questions, comments you may send correspondence
to. thegeminirisingrockinmachine@twc.com

Official Website
www.thegeminirisingrockinmachine.com

Fuckaholic is a collection of Mind Rockin' songs that needed to be created for their induction into The Book Of Bad Songs. There will... Might be different volumes for The Book Of Bad Songs, however there is... Will be a constant between them. This constant is that every Mind Rockin' song that makes it into The Book Of Bad Songs is a Mind Rockin' song that someone will hate and someone else will love.

If the word Fuck bothers you, then flip to page? Well Fuck, I guess just forget about it, for the word Fuck is inside this book a lot. Because Fuckaholic is a book that consists of Mind Rockin' songs about Fucking and being Fucked over.

I've brought to your Mind Rockin' Minds in the past, Mind Rockin' songs consisting of Love, Sexy, Political, Social, Fantasy and Horror. Now it is time to really say Fuck It, life is too short not to have a little fun. This book is for those that want to laugh and say that is Bad, over and over again. Because life and the World is too Heavy not to say Fuck It.

Are you ready Mind Rockers?

Let's say it one more time...

Fuck It!

Peace and Enjoy,

The Gemini Rising Rockin' Machine

I almost forgot the great news...

Thirty six Mind Rockin' songs out of all the seventy four Mind Rockin' songs that are included in this book has the word Fuck in its title... Imagine that Mind Rockers.

Fuckaholic - The Book Of Bad Songs
(Pages 04-54)

(Side One)
Fuckaholic (710.)
Lunch Fuck (911.)
Beer And Weed (874.)
Let's Fuck First (875.)
Drawer Buddie (893.)

(Side Two)
Tear It Up (44.)
Bust (A Hell Of A Nut) (48.)
Party And Fuck (60.)
Lady Lust (15.)
I Love Them Women (62.)

(Side Three)
Horny Bastard (895.1)
I Got It Going On (894.1)
Quick And Easy (886.1)
Fuck My Boner (908.1)
Fucked By Me (961.1)

(Side Four)
Weed Whores (890.)
Hey Dumb Fucks (899.)
The Pissed Off Pothead (999.)
We Could Say Fuck It (1000.)
Let's Say Fuck It (1001.)

(Side Five)
Let's Get High And Fuck (16.)
Drunk Fucks #1 & Drunk Fucks #2 (19.)
Stuff Duck And A Blow Job (17.)
Fucking Is Fun (964.)
I'll Fuck You (965.1)

(Side Six)
I Am Who I Am (904.)
Both Of Them (876.)
Sucks In A Good Way (891.)
Man-Size Full-Sized (905.)
What I Did For Your Woman (727.)

(Side Seven)
T-Shirt And Panties (822.)
Lipstick On My Dick (823.1)
Pay Me First (824.)
Cheating Lady (828.)
Buy Me A Beer (You Bastard) (889.) {Original Version}
Buy Me A Beer (You Bastard) (889.1) {New Version}

(Side Eight)
I'm Dead And Horny (848.)
Psycho Lady (898.)
Screaming Sally (112.) {Original Version}
Screaming Sally (112.1) {New Version}
Snake Skin Lady Of The Night (812.)
Demon Goat Lady (811.)

Fuckaholic (710.)

I'm a Fucking – Fuckaholic
I-Fuck – All-The-Fucking-Time
I'm a Fucking – Fuckaholic
Looking-For a Fuck to Fuck-Tonight

I'm a Fucking – Fuckaholic
I'll-Fuck – Any-Fine-Around
I'm a Fucking – Fuckaholic
If-She's-Legal and Says-Yes
She's-The-Fuck – For-Me

(Chorus)
Fuckaholic – I'll Show The World
What Fucking Is All About
Fuckaholic – Fucking All The Way
Every Fucking Day
Fuckaholic – Would You Like To Fuck Me
I'm Free And Ready To Fuck Right Away

I'm a Fucking – Fuckaholic
I-Fuck – All-The-Fucking-Time
I'm a Fucking – Fuckaholic
Looking-For a Fuck to Fuck-Tonight

I'm a Fucking – Fuckaholic
I-Don't-Care – If-You-Fucking-Like-Me
I'm a Fucking – Fuckaholic
You-Can-Go – Fuck-Yourself
If-You-Think – I-Don't-Have-The-Right to Fuck

(Chorus)
Fuckaholic – I'll Show The World
What Fucking Is All About
Fuckaholic – Fucking All The Way
Every Fucking Day
Fuckaholic – Would You Like To Fuck Me
I'm Free And Ready To Fuck Right Away

Lunch Fuck (911.)

Baby – I'm-Horny-Hungry
All-The – Sexy-Time
I-Have-My – Breakfast-Fuck
I-Have-My – Dinner-Fuck

Baby-What-I-Need – From-You
Oh-So-Much – Is-For-You
To-Be-My – Lunch-Fuck

(Chorus)
Come On Sexy Baby – Be My Lunch Fuck
Come On Sexy Baby – Be My Lunch Fuck
Come On Sexy Baby – Let's Lunch Fuck Everyday

Baby – I'm-Horny-Hungry
All-The – Sexy-Time
I-Have-My – Breakfast-Fuck
I-Have-My – Dinner-Fuck

Baby-What-I-Need – From-You
Oh-So-Much – Is-For-You
To-Be-My – Lunch-Fuck

(Chorus)
Come On Sexy Baby – Be My Lunch Fuck
Come On Sexy Baby – Be My Lunch Fuck
Come On Sexy Baby – Let's Lunch Fuck Everyday

Baby – What's-On-The-Menu – Today
Lunch-Fucking – That's-What
Baby – What's-On-The-Menu – Tomorrow
Lunch-Fucking – That's-What
Baby – What's-On-The-Menu – Next-Week
Lunch-Fucking – That's-What
Don't-Worry-Baby – I-Won't-Tell-Nobody
That-You're-My – Lunch-Fuck – Not-Even
My-Breakfast-Fuck or My-Dinner-Fuck

Beer And Weed (874.)

What-The-Fuck – Is-Going-On
My-Mind's – All-Fucked-Up
From-Listening to Your-Endless-Shit

So-Fuck – The-Fuck-Off
Listen to Your-Own-Shit
Better-Yet – Just-Eat-It and Like-It

(Chorus)
I Need Beer And Weed
Because You're Making My Mind Bleed
I Need Beer And Weed
Because You're So Fucked Up
I Need Beer And Weed
Because You're Making My Mind Bleed
And Because I Like To Get Stoned And Drunk

What-The-Fuck – Is-Going-On
I'm-All-Fucked-Up and You're-Still-Around
Damn – Don't-You-Ever – Shut-The-Fuck-Up

You're-Like a Dog – That-Never-Stops-Barking
Because-You're – Tied-Up-Too-Tight
That-You-Can't – Lick-Your-Balls and Ass

Damn – That's – Bad
Guess-What – You-Fucked-Up-Fucker

(Chorus)
I Need Beer And Weed
Because You're Making My Mind Bleed
I Need Beer And Weed
Because You're So Fucked Up
I Need Beer And Weed
Because You're Making My Mind Bleed
And Because I Like To Get Stoned And Drunk

Let's Fuck First (875.)

I-Like-Your-Eyes – I-Like-Your-Lips
Wow – What a Pair of Hips
We-Could-Go-Dancing – We-Could-Talk
Both-Would-Be – Nice and Fun
But-That's – The-Problem-Baby
I'm-Wanting to Do – Something-Else-First

(Pre-Chorus)
I Tell You What – How About This Baby
Let's Fuck First – Then Talk About Dancing
In-Between Our Second Fucking

(Chorus)
Let's Fuck – Let's Fuck First
I'm Ready – You're Willing – So Baby
Let's Fuck – Let's Fuck First
I'm Hard – You're Wet – So Baby
Let's Fuck – Let's Fuck First

I-Like-Your-Eyes – I-Like-Your-Lips
Wow – What a Pair of Hips
We-Could-Go-Dancing – We-Could-Talk
Both-Would-Be – Nice and Fun
But-That's – The-Problem-Baby
I'm-Wanting to Do – Something-Else-First

(Pre-Chorus)
I Tell You What – How About This Baby
Let's Fuck First – Then Talk About Dancing
In-Between Our Second Fucking

(Chorus)
Let's Fuck – Let's Fuck First
I'm Ready – You're Willing – So Baby
Let's Fuck – Let's Fuck First
I'm Hard – You're Wet – So Baby
Let's Fuck – Let's Fuck First

Drawer Buddie (893.)

Happy-Days – Sad-Days
Good-Dates – Bad-Dates
Is-He-Fulfilling-Your – Special-Needs

Don't-Worry – Help-Is on The-Way
Something-That's – Out of Sight
Is-Rocketing to You – For-Extreme
Hours and Hours of Pleasure

(Chorus)
Drawer Buddie
Is A Lady's Best Friend
That Never Says No
I Can't Go Again
Drawer Buddie
Is A Lady's Best Friend
That Never Ever
Burbs And Farts

Happy-Days – Sad-Days
Good-Dates – Bad-Dates
Is-He-Fulfilling-Your – Special-Needs

Push-The-Blue-Button – For-Length
Push-The-Red-Button – For-Width
Don't-Be-Shy – Don't-Fear-Their-Hate
You-Are-Woman – You-Have-The-Right to Moan

(Chorus)
Drawer Buddie
Is A Lady's Best Friend
That Never Says No
I Can't Go Again
Drawer Buddie
Is A Lady's Best Friend
That Never Ever
Burbs And Farts

Tear It Up (44.)

Hey-Sexy – Why-You-Crying
Your-Man – Not-Getting-You-Off
I-Know-You – Don't-Know-Me
If-You-Promise-Sexy – Not to Fall
In-Love-With-Me – I'll-Do-Something
That-You'll – Never-Forget
Let-Me – Sing-It to You-Sexy

(Chorus)
Tear It Up – Woo Baby
I'll Tear Your Fineness Up
Tear It Up – Woo Baby
Tear You Up – Until You Can't Take It Any More
Tear It Up – Woo Baby
Tear You Up – 'Til You Scream More
Tear It Up – Woo Baby
Tear You Up – Leave You Begging For More
As I leave You Moaning – On Your Bed Or Floor

Hey-Sexy – Why-You-Crying
Your-Man – Not-Getting-You-Off
I-Know-You – Don't-Know-Me
If-You-Promise-Sexy – Not to Fall
In-Love-With-Me – I'll-Do-Something
That-You'll – Never-Forget
Let-Me – Sing-It to You-Sexy

(Chorus)
Tear It Up – Woo Baby
I'll Tear Your Fineness Up
Tear It Up – Woo Baby
Tear You Up – Until You Can't Take It Any More
Tear It Up – Woo Baby
Tear You Up – 'Til You Scream More
Tear It Up – Woo Baby
Tear You Up – Leave You Begging For More
As I leave You Moaning – On Your Bed Or Floor

Bust (A Hell Of A Nut) (48.)

Come on Everybody
I-Can't-Be – The-Only-One
That-Likes to Bust
A-Hell of a Nut

What's so Good
About-Being-Mad – All-The-Time
Get-Off – Your-Ass
Flick – Your-Dick
Come on Stupid-Shit

(Chorus)
Bust
Bust A Hell Of A Nut
Bust
Bust A Hell Of A Nut
Bust
Bust A Hell Of A Nut

It's-Not – Hard to Do
When it's – Hard-For-You
The-Time is Now
For-You to Go – Balls-Out
Tear-It-Up – And
Bust a Hell – Of a Nut

Quivering and Shaking
Save – Your-Breath
You'll-Have – None-Left
When it's Time to

(Chorus)
Bust
Bust A Hell Of A Nut
Bust
Bust A Hell Of A Nut
Bust
Bust A Hell Of A Nut

Come on Everybody
I-Can't-Be – The-Only-One
That-Likes to Bust
A-Hell of a Nut

What's so Good
About-Being-Mad – All-The-Time
Get-Off – Your-Ass
Flick – Your-Dick
Come on Stupid-Shit

(Chorus)
Bust
Bust A Hell Of A Nut
Bust
Bust A Hell Of A Nut
Bust
Bust A Hell Of A Nut

It's-Not – Hard to Do
When it's Hard – For-You
The-Time is Now
For-You to Go – Balls-Out
Tear-It-Up – And
Bust a Hell – Of a Nut

Thank-You – Thank-You
Remember – It-Don't-Count
Unless-You – Flip-It-Twice
Makes-It so Nice
When-You – When-You

(Chorus)
Bust
Bust A Hell Of A Nut
Bust
Bust A Hell Of A Nut
Bust
Bust A Hell Of A Nut

Party And Fuck (60.)

What's – That-Sound
It's – All-Around
Sounds-Like – Partying to Me
Beer – Weed – Pussy
The-Three-Things – That-I-Need
When it's Time to Party and Fuck

Drink it Down
Squeeze – Some-Ass
Toke it Up
Get-My – Fingers-Damp

Baby-Take-That – Last-Sip
Then-Unzip – My-Pants
Be-Careful – No-Teeth
Just-In-Case – I-Choke-On-This-Toke

(Pre-Chorus)
What The Fuck Are You Waiting For
Beer – Weed and Pussy is Everywhere
It's Time To Party And Fuck

What The Fuck Are You Waiting For
Beer – Weed and Pussy is Everywhere
It's Time To Party And Fuck

(Chorus)
Come On Everybody
It's Time To Party And Fuck
Drink – Drink – Drink
Toke – Toke – Toke
Fuck – Fuck – Fuck
It's Time To Party And Fuck

Come On Everybody
It's Time To Party And Fuck
Let's Get Fucked Up
And Fuck Everything In Sight

Smell-All – The-Fuck-Weed
In-Here – Tonight
Pass-Me – That-Joint
Damn – I-Just-Spilled
My-Fucking – Beer

Drink it Down
Squeeze – Some-Ass
Toke it Up
Get-My – Fingers-Damp

Hey-Baby – You-Look so Fine
I'm-Drunk and High
I-Wanna-Fuck – Until-I-Pass-Out
Would-You – Like to Join-Me

(Pre-Chorus)
What The Fuck Are You Waiting For
Beer – Weed and Pussy is Everywhere
It's Time To Party And Fuck

What The Fuck Are You Waiting For
Beer – Weed and Pussy is Everywhere
It's Time To Party And Fuck

(Chorus)
Come On Everybody
It's Time To Party And Fuck
Drink – Drink – Drink
Toke – Toke – Toke
Fuck – Fuck – Fuck
It's Time To Party And Fuck

Come On Everybody
It's Time To Party And Fuck
Let's Get Fucked Up
And Fuck Everything In Sight

Lady Lust (15.)

Lady-Lust
Gives-Me – All-That-I-Need
She's-Here to Please
Lady-Lust
When-I'm-Up – She-Sits-Atop of Me
When-I'm-Down – She-Goes-Down on Me

Lady-Lust
The-Sun-Rises and Sets – In-My-Pants
Knees on The-Floor – Licking-Her-Lips
Lady-Lust
I'm a Greedy-Bastard
I-Always – Want-More

(Chorus)
My Lady Lust
The Face Of An Angel
The Body Of A Slut
My Lady Lust
Let's Me Fuck Her
All I Want

Lady-Lust
You're-All – That-I-Need
Don't-Matter – If-You're-Bad-For-Me

Lady-Lust
She's-Got-Me – By-The-Balls
She-Makes-My – Wallet-Thinner
But-I-Don't – Give a Fuck

(Chorus)
My Lady Lust
The Face Of An Angel
The Body Of A Slut
My Lady Lust
Let's Me Fuck Her
All I Want

I Love Them Women (62.)

I-Love – Them-Women
That-Love to Love-Me
Yes-Indeed
I-Love – Them-Women
All-Dressed-Up – Looking so Fine
Yes-Indeed

(Chorus)
I Love Them Women
That Have Everything I Want
I Love Them Women
That Are Willing To Put Out
I Love Them Women
That Brings A Girlfriend With Them

I-Love – Them-Women
That-Bounces it All-In-My-Face
Bounce-Them – Away-Baby
I-Love – Them-Women
That-Love to Go-Down on Me
Don't-Forget to Breathe – Baby

(Chorus)
I Love Them Women
That Have Everything I Want
I Love Them Women
That Are Willing To Put Out
I Love Them Women
That Brings A Girlfriend With Them

I-Love – Them-Women
That-Like to Fuck – All-Night
I-Love – Them-Women
Because-Fucking is All-I'm-About
And-There's – Nothing-Wrong-With-That

(Repeat Chorus)

Horny Bastard (895.1.)

Yes-Sweet-Lady – Take-It-Off
I'm-Always-Ready to Fuck
Save-Your-Name – Baby
For-When-I'm – Putting-My-Clothes-Back-On

Let's-Go – We-Haven't – Got-Time to Waste
Smile-Baby – While-You-Lay-Down or Bend-Over
'Cause-Baby – I'm-Ready to Fuck-You – Anyway-You-Want

(Chorus)
I'm Blessed – I'm Damned
I'm-Horny – I'm a Bastard
I'm The Horny Bastard
That Wants To Fuck You
I'm Blessed – I'm Damned
I'm-Horny – I'm a Bastard
I'm The Horny Bastard
That Wants To Fuck You

Yes-Sweet-Lady – Take-It-Off
I'm-Always-Ready to Fuck
Save-Your-Name – Baby
For-When-I'm – Putting-My-Clothes-Back-On

Let's-Go – We-Haven't – Got-Time to Waste
Smile-Baby – While-You-Lay-Down or Bend-Over
'Cause-Baby – I'm-Ready to Fuck-You – Anyway-You-Want

(Chorus)
I'm Blessed – I'm Damned
I'm-Horny – I'm a Bastard
I'm The Horny Bastard
That Wants To Fuck You
I'm Blessed – I'm Damned
I'm-Horny – I'm a Bastard
I'm The Horny Bastard
That Wants To Fuck You

I Got It Going On (894.1.)

My-Lovers – Have-Became so Harsh
They-Won't – Fuck-Me-Anymore
I-Come a Knock-Knock – Knocking
On-Their-Doors
They-Yell-This – Out to Me

Go-Away – Horny-Bastard
You-Ain't – Fucking-Me-No-More
Our-Legs – Are-Closed to You
Now-Get-Going – Horny-Bastard
Damn – I-Guess-They-Figured-Me-Out

(Chorus)
Hey-Hey – What A Day – I Got It Going On
Between My Legs – Yeah
Hey-Hey – What A Day – I Got It Going On
Between My Legs – Yeah
And That's All I Have To Say – Hey

Hitting – The-Road
No-Use-In – Sticking-Around
'Cause-The-Well – Has-Gone-Dry
New-Town – New-Tits and Asses
I-Guess-I'll – Start-Fucking-The-Finest
'Til-They-Figure-Me-Out – 'Til-I-Hear

Go-Away – Horny-Bastard
You-Ain't – Fucking-Me-No-More
Our-Legs – Are-Closed to You
Now-Get-Going – Horny-Bastard
Damn – I-Guess-They-Figured-Me-Out

(Chorus)
Hey-Hey – What A Day – I Got It Going On
Between My Legs – Yeah
Hey-Hey – What A Day – I Got It Going On
Between My Legs – Yeah
And That's All I Have To Say – Hey

Quick And Easy (886.1.)

Nice to Meet-You – Tonight
Tasting-You is Out of Sight
First-Touch – Made-Me-Hard
Straight-Between – My-Legs
Now it's Time – For-Fucking

Sit on Top of Me
Bite – My-Ass
I-Like – Everything
Believe-Me-Baby – We'll-Enjoy-Ourselves

(Chorus)
I Like to Rock – I Like to Fuck
I Like It – I Like It
Quick And Easy
Come On Baby – Quick And Easy
Let's Fuck And Finish
So We Can Fuck Again
Oh Yes Baby – Again After That Too

Give-Me a Minute-Baby
I-Need a Beer and My-Pipe
That's it Sexy-Baby
Lick-Me – From-Head to Toe

It's-Been a Long – Long-Day
Your-Loving – With-All the Extras
Gives-My-Mind – Something to Think-About
Like-Staying – All-Night-Long

(Chorus)
I Like to Rock – I Like to Fuck
I Like It – I Like It
Quick And Easy
Come On Baby – Quick And Easy
Let's Fuck And Finish
So We Can Fuck Again
Oh Yes Baby – Again After That Too

Fuck My Boner (908.1.)

I-Could-Tell-You – My-Sign
I-Could-Tell-You – My-Favorite-Color
I-Could-Even – Tell-You – My-Name
But-That's-Not – My-Style – No – Not-At-All

My-Style-Baby – Is-Fucking-All-Night-Long
So-What – Do-You-Say – Baby
Do-You-Want-To – Fuck My Boner

(Chorus)
Come On Baby – Fuck My Boner
It's Such A Great Boner To Fuck
Come On Baby – Fuck My Boner
If You Say No Baby – I'll Let
Some Other Hottie – Fuck My Boner
So Come On Baby – Fuck My Boner
Before You Lose Your Chance
At Fucking The Perfect Boner

I-Could-Tell-You – My-Sign
I-Could-Tell-You – My-Favorite-Color
I-Could-Even – Tell-You – My-Name
But-That's-Not – My-Style – No – Not-At-All

My-Style-Baby – Is-Fucking-All-Night-Long
So-What – Do-You-Say – Baby
Do-You-Want-To – Fuck My Boner

(Chorus)
Come On Baby – Fuck My Boner
It's Such A Great Boner To Fuck
Come On Baby – Fuck My Boner
If You Say No Baby – I'll Let
Some Other Hottie – Fuck My Boner
So Come On Baby – Fuck My Boner
Before You Lose Your Chance
At Fucking The Perfect Boner

Fucked By Me (961.1.)

I'm-Thick and Hard
I-Fit – Into-Place – Just-Right
Ask – Around
I'm a Hell – Of a Fuck

I-Know – We-Just-Met
But-Baby – I-Have-The-Bed
If-You – Got-The-Time

(Chorus)
What Do You Say Sexy
Do You Have The Time
To Get Fucked By Me
I Have A Couple Of Hours
Why Not Get Fucked By Me
I'm A Hell Of A Fuck
That You Can Brag About Later
To Your Friends And Strangers Alike

Sexy – After-We're-Done
Try-Your-Best – Not to Fall in Love
Believe-Me – When-I-Say
I've-Been-There – Many-Times

Still-I-Know – We-Just-Met
But-Baby – I-Have-The-Bed
If-You – Got-The-Time

(Chorus)
What Do You Say Sexy
Do You Have The Time
To Get Fucked By Me
I Have A Couple Of Hours
Why Not Get Fucked By Me
I'm A Hell Of A Fuck
You Can Brag About Later
To Your Friends And Strangers Alike

Weed Whores (890.)

Mother-Earth – Grows it For-Free
For-All-Mammals and Animals
This is Lost to You
Why – I'll-Tell-You-Why

You're a Weed-Whore
Because-You-Charge
Way-Too-Fucking-Much – For-Weed
Shame-On-You – For-Not-Remembering
What-The-Past-Was-Like – For-All of Us

(Chorus)
Weed Whores Everywhere I Look
Damn Fucking Shame
It's Finally Legal Here And There
And You Charge Everyone More
Then They Can Buy It On The Streets
What The Fuck's Wrong With You
You Sorry Ass Weed Whores

I-Can-Understand – The-Man
But-You – Damn-Weed-Whores
You're-Suppose to Be-Better
But-You're-Not – So-You-Suck

I-Hope-Your-Buds – Turn to Shake
I-Hope-Your-Funk – Turns to Bunk
I-Hope-You-Become – Allergic to Weed
Because-You're-Nothing-But – Weed-Whores

(Chorus)
Weed Whores Everywhere I Look
Damn Fucking Shame
It's Finally Legal Here And There
And You Charge Everyone More
Then They Can Buy It On The Streets
What The Fuck's Wrong With You
You Sorry Ass Weed Whores

Hey Dumb Fucks (899.)

Dumb-Fucks – Wants-Everything-For-Free
Dumb-Fucks – Dumb-Fucks
Wants-To-Bring – Out-Their-Hate
Dumb-Fucks – Believes-The-Man-Loves-Them
Dumb-Fucks – Dumb-Fucks
Will-Follow – The-Man
All-The-Way to Their-Deaths

(Chorus)
Hey Dumb Fucks
Why Don't You Believe in Freedom
Hey Dumb Fucks
Why Don't You Believe In Peace
Hey Dumb Fucks
Why Don't You Believe In Love
Hey Dumb Fucks
Stop Being Dumb Fucks
Before You Kill Somebody

Dumb-Fucks – Wants-Everything-For-Free
Dumb-Fucks – Dumb-Fucks
Wants-To-Bring – Out-Their-Hate
Dumb-Fucks – Believes-The-Man-Loves-Them
Dumb-Fucks – Dumb-Fucks
Will-Follow – The-Man
All-The-Way to Their-Deaths

(Chorus)
Hey Dumb Fucks
Why Don't You Believe in Freedom
Hey Dumb Fucks
Why Don't You Believe In Peace
Hey Dumb Fucks
Why Don't You Believe In Love
Hey Dumb Fucks
Stop Being Dumb Fucks
Before You Kill Somebody

The Pissed Off Pothead (999.)

I'm a Mellow-Guy
That-Likes to Get-High
Mother-Earth's – Finest
Is-My-Choice in Life
That-I-Only-Smoke – With-The-Cool

Don't-Look at Me – Like-That
I-Just-Smoke Weed – I-Don't
Kill – Rape or Destroy
That's-You-World – Every-Day
While-I'm-Trying to Be-Safe
While-I'm-Trying to Get-High in Peace

(Chorus)
Damn You World – I'm a Mellow Guy
Now-I'm – The Pissed Off Pothead
Damn You World – I Just Like To Smoke Weed
Now-I'm – The Pissed Off Pothead
You Made Me So Mad World
That I'd Rather Fuck With You Now
Instead Of Getting High – Stupid Fucking World

You-Keep on Messing-With-Me
While-I'm-Trying to Get-High
I've-Had-Enough of Your-Bunk
While-I'm-Toking on My-Funk
You-Really-Hurt – My-Feelings
When-You-Bust-Me – Instead of a Killer
You-Really-Hurt – My-Feelings
When-I-Get-More-Time – Than a Rapist

I-Just-Smoke Weed – What's-Wrong-With-You
The-Way-I-See-It – You-Just-Don't-Know-Any-Better
What-Choice-Do-I-Have – I-Have to Tell-You-This
The-Only-Time – You-Ever-Pleased a Lady
Is-When-You – Gave-Them a Big-Thick-Tip

(Repeat Chorus)

We Could Say Fuck It (1000.)

The World – Likes to Bleed
Actually-That's – Humanity
Fucked-Up – Ain't-It – I'm-Human
You're-Human – They're-Not-Anymore

Old-Fashion-Ways is Killing-The-World
Can't-Wash-Away – All its Sins
I-Don't-Really – Feel-Like it Either
I've-Got-Better-Things to Do
Like-Help – Like-Save – Like-Change-The-World

(Chorus)
We Could Say Fuck It
It's A Really Easy Thing To Do
We Could Say Fuck It
Let The World Save Itself
We Could Say Fuck It
Do Nothing But Complain
About All The Fucked Up Shit
We Could Say Fuck It
But That Would Be
A Stupid Fucking Thing To Do

The-World – Can't-Save Itself
That's-Really a Fucking-Big-One
To-Start-Off-With – Check-This-Out
We-Sign a Pledge – We-Change-The-World
The-Three-No's is What it's All-About

One – I-Won't-Kill / Two – I-Won't-Rape
Three – I-Won't-Take – The-Innocence of a Child
Really-Fucking-Simple a Trained-Dog-Could-Do-It
Listen-Up – Fuck-Your-Feelings
Bleeding and Dying – Are-Much-Worse
Fuck-It – Let's-Start-The-Three-Up
Let's-Help – Let's-Save – Let's-Change-The-World

(Repeat Chorus)

Let's Say Fuck It (1001.)

Fuck-Me – Fuck-You
Fuck-This – Fuck-That
Everything's-Fucked – Everything's-Crazy
I-Don't-Want to Kill
This-Fucked-Up-World – Won't-Make-Me
Never-Mind – Let's-Change-The-Subject

(Chorus #1)
Let's Say Fuck It
It's Really Easy To Do
Let's Say Fuck It
Let The World Kill Itself
While We Throw A Party

Fuck-The-People – Why
You-Fucking – Tell-Me-Why
Because-I-Fucking – Don't-Know-Why
I-Do-Know – This is Fucking-Boring
Do-You-Want to Talk – About-Killing-Again
Never-Mind – Let's-Change – The-Subject

(Chorus #2)
Let's Say Fuck It
It's Really Easy To Do
Let's Say Fuck It
Let The World Fuck Itself
While We Have An Orgy

Fuck-Me – Fuck-You
Fuck-This – Fuck-That
Everything's-Fucked – Everything's-Crazy
Fuck-The-People – Why
You-Fucking – Tell-Me-Why
Because-I-Fucking – Don't-Know-Why
Never-Mind – Let's-Change – The-Subject

(Repeat Chorus #1 & Chorus #2)

Let's Get High And Fuck (16.)

Hey-Baby – I-Got a Fat-Sack
I'll-Start-Rolling a Log
You-Start-Taking-Off – Your-Clothes

Now-That-I – Think-About-It – Baby
Why-Don't-You – Call-Your-Sexy-Friend
I-Bet-She'll-Enjoy – Getting-High and Fucked

(Chorus)
Let's Get High And Fuck
Nothing Can Compare To
Toking It Up And Fucking Away
Let's Get High And Fuck
Nothing Can Compare To
Toking It Up And Fucking Away
Let's Get High And Fuck
Nothing Can Compare To
Toking It Up And Fucking Away

Ladies – I'm-Fried and Tired
I'll-Roll-Up – Another-Log
Why-Don't-The-Two of You – Keep-Going-On

Wow-Ladies – Save-Some-For-Me
Would-You-Like-Me to Order a Pizza
Here-Toke-This – While-I-Make-The-Call
Anybody-Got-Any-Cash – I'm-Broke – But-I'm-Hung

(Chorus)
Let's Get High And Fuck
Nothing Can Compare To
Toking It Up And Fucking Away
Let's Get High And Fuck
Nothing Can Compare To
Toking It Up And Fucking Away
Let's Get High And Fuck
Nothing Can Compare To
Toking It Up And Fucking Away

The-Sun is Coming-Up
My-Sack is Depleted
My-Dick is Numb
What a Night-Ladies
Same-Time – Tonight

Don't-Worry – Sexy-Ladies
My-Sack – Will-Be-Thick
My-Dick – Will-Be-Hard
Just-Like – Last-Night

(Chorus)
Let's Get High And Fuck
Nothing Can Compare To
Toking It Up And Fucking Away
Let's Get High And Fuck
Nothing Can Compare To
Toking It Up And Fucking Away
Let's Get High And Fuck
Nothing Can Compare To
Toking It Up And Fucking Away

Hey-Baby – I-Got a Fat-Sack
I'll-Start-Rolling a Log
You-Start-Taking-Off – Your-Clothes

Now-That-I – Think-About-It – Baby
Why-Don't-You – Call-Your-Sexy-Friend
I-Bet-She'll-Enjoy – Getting-High and Fucked

(Chorus)
Let's Get High And Fuck
Nothing Can Compare To
Toking It Up And Fucking Away
Let's Get High And Fuck
Nothing Can Compare To
Toking It Up And Fucking Away
Let's Get High And Fuck
Nothing Can Compare To
Toking It Up And Fucking Away

Drunk Fucks #1 (19.)

It's-Late – Too-Much-Partying
Now-It's-Time to Find-Someone
To-Hug – Kiss and Fuck
Damn-It to Hell – I-Fucked-Up-Again

Can't-Be – Too-Picky
If-I-Want to Get-Laid
Maybe-I'll-Learn – My-Lesson
Someday – To-Fuck – Then-Drink
Instead of Drinking – Then-Fucking

(Chorus)
I Guess That Is What I Get
For Not Thinking With The Right Head
It's All My Fault – I Wanted A Fine Woman
Now All There's Left Is
A Bunch Of Drunk Fucks
That I Don't Want To Fuck

It's-Late – Too-Much-Partying
Now-It's-Time to Find-Someone
To-Hug – Kiss and Fuck
Damn-It to Hell – I-Fucked-Up-Again

Can't-Be – Too-Picky
If-I-Want to Get-Laid
Maybe-I'll-Learn – My-Lesson
Someday – To-Fuck – Then-Drink
Instead of Drinking – Then-Fucking

(Chorus)
I Guess That Is What I Get
For Not Thinking With The Right Head
It's All My Fault – I Wanted A Fine Woman
Now All That Is Left
Is A Bunch Of Drunk Fucks
That I Don't Want To Fuck

Drunk Fucks #2

It's-Late – Too-Much-Saying-No
Now-It's-Time to Find-Someone
To-Take – Me-Home
Damn-It to Hell – I-Fucked-Up-Again

Can't-Be – Too-Picky
If-I-Want to Get-Laid
Maybe-I'll-Learn – My-Lesson
Someday – To-Fuck – Then-Drink
Instead of Drinking – Then-Fucking

(Chorus)
I Guess That Is What I Get
For Playing Hard To Get
It's All My Fault – I Wanted A Fine Man
Now All There's Left Is
A Bunch Of Drunk Fucks
That I Don't Want Fucking Me

It's-Late – Too-Much-Saying-No
Now-It's-Time to Find-Someone
To-Take – Me-Home
Damn-It to Hell – I-Fucked-Up-Again

Can't-Be – Too-Picky
If-I-Want to Get-Laid
Maybe-I'll-Learn – My-Lesson
Someday – To-Fuck – Then-Drink
Instead of Drinking – Then-Fucking

(Chorus)
I Guess That Is What I Get
For Playing Hard To Get
It's All My Fault – I Wanted A Fine Man
Now All There's Left Is
A Bunch Of Drunk Fucks
That I Don't Want Fucking Me

Stuff Duck And A Blow Job (17.)

When-I-Come-Home – Tired as Hell
From a Hard-Day's-Work
All-I-Want is Two-Things
Stuff-Duck And a Blow-Job

I-Want-It – Crispy and Tasty
I-Want-It – Deep and Wild
I-Want-Them-Both – Wet and Juicy

(Chorus)
Do It For Me Darling
Stuff It And Suck It
Oh Yeah Baby
Stuff Duck And A Blow Job
Do It For Me Darling
Stuff It And Suck It
Stuff Duck And A Blow Job
That Is What I Want From You Baby

When-I-Come-Home – Tired as Hell
From a Hard-Day's-Work
All-I-Want is Two-Things
Stuff-Duck And a Blow-Job

I-Want-It – Crispy and Tasty
I-Want-It – Deep and Wild
I-Want-Them-Both – Wet and Juicy

(Chorus)
Do It For Me Darling
Stuff It And Suck It
Oh Yeah Baby
Stuff Duck And A Blow Job
Do It For Me Darling
Stuff It And Suck It
Stuff Duck And A Blow Job
That Is What I Want From You Baby

Fucking Is Fun (964.)

It's-Easy to Hate – It's-Easy to Kill
It's-Not-Easy to Love – With-All-Your-Heart
I-Say-Fuck-It – One-Life – What-Can
One-Do – But-Try to Live-Another-Day

I'll-Tell-You-What – You-Can-Try-Fucking
That's-Right – You-Want to Know-Why
It's-Very-Simple – Fucking-Is-Fun

(Chorus)
Come On You Non-Fucking
Try Some Fucking
Because Fucking Is Fun
That's Why I Do It All The Time
Come On You Non-Fucking
Try Some Fucking
Because Fucking Is Fun
That's Why I Do It All The Time

It's-Easy to Hate – It's-Easy to Kill
It's-Not-Easy to Love – With-All-Your-Heart
I-Say-Fuck-It – One-Life – What-Can
One-Do – But-Try to Live-Another-Day

I'll-Tell-You-What – You-Can-Try-Fucking
That's-Right – You-Want to Know-Why
It's-Very-Simple – Fucking-Is-Fun

(Chorus)
Come On You Non-Fucking
Try Some Fucking
Because Fucking Is Fun
That's Why I Do It All The Time
Come On You Non-Fucking
Try Some Fucking
Because Fucking Is Fun
That's Why I Do It All The Time

I'll Fuck You (965.1.)

Sorry-Sexy – You're-Incredible
But-I'm – Not-Looking
For-Love – Tonight
Been-There – Done-That
Many – Many-Times

If-You-Got-The-Time – Sexy-Incredible
I'd-Love to Tell-You
What-I-Like to Do – Tonight

(Chorus)
Sexy Incredible – If You Let Me
I'll Fuck You
Like You've Never
Been Fucked Before
Just Say Yes
Sexy Incredible
I'll Fuck You
Right Here – Right Now

Sexy-Incredible – Thanks-For
Slapping-My-Face – Instead of
Kicking-Me – In-My-Balls

Let-Me – Try-This-Again
If-You-Got-The-Time – Sexy-Incredible
I'd-Love to Tell-You
What-I-Like to Do – Tonight

(Chorus)
Sexy Incredible – If You Let Me
I'll Fuck You
Like You've Never
Been Fucked Before
Just Say Yes
Sexy Incredible
I'll Fuck You
Right Here – Right Now

I Am Who I Am (904.)

Baby – I-Miss-Your-Body
I-Know – I-Cheated on You
But-That-Was a Month-Ago

I've-Changed – Baby-Believe-Me
Look-Into-My-Eyes – Feel in My-Soul
See a Man – That-Wants-You-Back
In-His – Bed-Tonight

(Chorus)
I Am Who I Am
Baby You Know This
I Am Who I Am
Told You From The Start
That I Was A Cheater
I Am Who I Am
I Ain't Never Going To Change
I Am Who I Am
Just Be Happy To Have Your Turn

Baby – It's-Time to Forgive-Me
Baby – It's-Time for Kissing and Hugging
Baby – It's-Time to Fuck

Then-I-Have to Split – I'll be Back-In a Day
Just-Stay – Right-Where-You-Are
When-I-Get-Back – We'll-Fuck-Again

(Chorus)
I Am Who I Am
Baby You Know This
I Am Who I Am
Told You From The Start
That I Was A Cheater
I Am Who I Am
I Ain't Never Going To Change
I Am Who I Am
Baby Just Be Happy To Have Your Turn

Both Of Them (876.)

I-Have-Two-Houses – I-Have-Two-Cars
I'm-Two-Faced and Horny
Looking-For a Great-Time

How-Are-You-Sexy – You and Your-Friend
Ready to Share-Me
I'll-Let the Both of You – Decide
Who – Goes – First

(Chorus)
Let's Hear It For Me, Myself & I
Once Again Tonight – Like Fate
I Get To Have Two At A Time
Even Better – They Always Change
Every Night – A Brand New
Two At A Time To Enjoy
While I Always Stay The Same
Hard And Hung – Sexy Warrior

I'm So Happy – Let's-Take a Walk
Let's-Lay on The-Floor
Yes of Course – The-Both of You
I'm-Never a One on One

Don't-Fight – Who-Ever-Gets-Second-Time
Will-Get-It – Just as Good
Don't-Believe-Me – Well-Then-I-Guess
I-Have-To-Let-It – All-Hang-Out

(Chorus)
Let's Hear It For Me, Myself & I
Once Again Tonight – Like Fate
I Get To Have Two At A Time
Even Better – They Always Change
Every Night – A Brand New
Two At A Time To Enjoy
While I Always Stay The Same
Hard And Hung – Sexy Warrior

Sucks In A Good Way (891.)

I-Tell-You-Man – Getting-Laid
Is-My-Life – I'm-Perfect at It
Would-You – Like to Watch
No-Charge – Maybe
You'll-Learn – Something

That's-Alright – I-Understand
But-Listen to This

(Chorus)
I'm A Lucky Man
Whose Ladies
Sucks In A Good Way
Yes That's Right
I'm A Lucky Man
Whose Ladies
Sucks In A Good Way
Don't You Wish You Were Me

Look at Your – Old-Lady
Not-Bad – Not-Bad
I-Think – She-Likes-Me
Give-Me – An-Hour-With-Her
I'll-Change-Her – Free of Charge

That's-Alright – I-Understand
But-Listen to This

(Chorus)
I'm A Lucky Man
Whose Ladies
Sucks In A Good Way
Yes That's Right
I'm A Lucky Man
Whose Ladies
Sucks In A Good Way
Don't You Wish You Were Me

Man-Size Full-Sized (908.)

I-Have a Lot of Bad-Habits
Oh – Yes – I – Do
This-Bothers-Me-Not – I'm-Not-Good
I'm-Great – And I'm-Always-Horny

Once a Night – Not-My-Style
Twice a Night – Not-Even-Close
Five-Times is Just-Right – Besides
I-Have to Get Some-Sleep – Sometimes
Oh – Yes – I – Do

(Chorus)
I'm A Man That Likes My
Man-Size Full-Sized
So Get Ready Baby
For Some Rocking And A Rolling
'Cause Baby – I'm A Man That Likes My
Man-Size Full-Sized – Every Night

I-Have a Lot of Bad-Habits
Oh – Yes – I – Do
This-Bothers-Me-Not – I'm-Not-Good
I'm-Great – And I'm-Always-Horny

Once a Night – Not-My-Style
Twice a Night – Not-Even-Close
Five-Times is Just-Right – Besides
I-Have to Get Some-Sleep – Sometimes
Oh – Yes – I – Do

(Chorus)
I'm A Man That Likes My
Man-Size Full-Sized
So Get Ready Baby
For Some Rocking And A Rolling
'Cause Baby – I'm A Man That Likes My
Man-Size Full-Sized – Every Night

What I Did For Your Woman (727.)

Freedom in My-Hands
Attitude in My-Pants
I-Feel so Alive
Tonight – I'm-Going to Party

Give-Me-One – Give-Me-Two
I'll-Take-Them-Both – At a Time
Turn-Your-Back – Walk-Away
I'll-Make – Your-Woman-Notice
What-I'll-Give-Her – Like-Only-I-Can-Give-Her

(Chorus)
Hate Me If You Want To
I Don't Give A Damn
I Just Fucked Your Woman
So Go Dumb-Ass Yourself Away
And Buy Me A Beer
For What I Did For Your Woman

Back-Off-Mr. Limpy – That-Can't-Party
Your-Hate is Blinding – Your-Mind
It's-Not-My-Fault – It's-Not-Her-Fault
It's-Your-Fault – That's-All

Can-I-Help-You – Why-Should-I
This is How – I-Make-My-Money
Check-Your-Account – Your-Woman is
Willing to Spend – Everything-You-Got
Just to Spend-Time – Being-Next to Living-Heaven

(Chorus)
Hate Me If You Want To
I Don't Give A Damn
I Just Fucked Your Woman
So Go Dumb-Ass Yourself Away
And Buy Me A Beer
For What I Did For Your Woman

T-Shirt And Panties (822.)

I'm-Leaving-Tonight – Baby
I'll be Gone – For-Awhile
When-I – Come-Back to You
Don't-Worry-About – Getting-All-Sexy

'Cause-Baby – All-I-Want – Is-To-See
You-In a T-Shirt and Panties – Let-Me-Sing
My-Song to You – Before-You – Tell-Me-Goodbye

(Chorus)
T-Shirt And Panties
That's My Wish Baby
T-Shirt And Panties
That's What I Want
Is To Come Home To You
While You're Wearing A
T-Shirt And Panties
Looking So Ready To Feed My Hunger

Thank-You-Baby – You-Look so Fine
In-Your – T-Shirt and Panties
Glad to Be-Home – I've-Missed-You so Much

Baby-Forget – My-Bags – My-Dinner
I-Love-You – I-Need-You
Let-Me-Sing – My-Song to You
One-More-Time – Before-We
Go to Bed and Say – Hello

(Chorus)
T-Shirt And Panties
That's My Wish Baby
T-Shirt And Panties
That's What I Want
Is To Come Home To You
While You're Wearing A
T-Shirt And Panties
Looking So Ready To Feed My Hunger

Lipstick On My Dick (823.1.)

Hey-Baby – I-Like-Your-Lips
Really-Dig – That-Color-Red
I'm-Fine – I'm-Horny – How-About-You
Let's-Talk – Let's-Take a Walk
Let's-Find – Privacy-Real-Quick

(Pre-Chorus)
Baby Oh Baby – That's It
Don't Worry One Little Bit
That You're Getting Lipstick On My Dick
It Looks Real Good – All Red Like That

(Chorus)
Baby That's It – Keep On Getting
Lipstick On My Dick
Then Bend Over Real Quick
'Cause I Got Some Dick
To Give To You – With Lipstick On It

No-Baby – I'll-Follow-You
Want to Get a Better – Look at That-Ass
Wow-Baby – Your-Ass is First-Class
Baby – I-Want-You to Do-Something-First
With-Those – Red-Sexy-Lips of Yours

(Pre-Chorus)
Baby Oh Baby – That's It
Don't Worry One Little Bit
That You're Getting Lipstick On My Dick
It Looks Real Good – All Red Like That

(Chorus)
Baby That's It – Keep On Getting
Lipstick On My Dick
Then Bend Over Real Quick
'Cause I Got Some Dick
To Give To You – With Lipstick On It

Pay Me First (824.)

When-You're – All-Alone
With a Body – That is So-Lonely
Don't-Hesitate – Call-Me

I'll-Make-Your-Sad – Happy
I'll-Make-Your-Wanting – Satisfied
I'm-Every-Woman's – Sexual-Desire
After – I'm-Paid-First

(Chorus)
Yes You Can Touch It
Go Ahead – Take A Feel
Of What You Want So Badly
Okay Baby – Reality Time
Pay Me First
Then You Can Enjoy It
However You Want

Baby – Your-Time is Up
It-Will – Cost-Extra
If-You-Want-It – Long-Again

Please-No-Begging – Please-No-Crying
They-Will-Do-You – No-Good-Baby
Believe-Me – I've-Heard It All-Before

I-Have a Saying – That-Goes-Like-This
Take-Your-Wallet – Back-Out
So-I-Can – Explain-It to You

(Chorus)
Yes You Can Touch It
Go Ahead – Take A Feel
Of What You Want So Badly
Okay Baby – Reality Time
Pay Me First
Then You Can Enjoy It
However You Want

Cheating Lady (828.)

Way-Down in Horny-Ville
That's-Where – My-Lady-Sins
This-I – Never-Knew
Until-I – Felt-Its-Blade
Like a Knife – In-My-Back

What a Crying-Shame
She's to Blame – For-Sure
What-Can-I-Do – I-Think-I-Got-It

(Chorus)
I'm Going To Drop My Cheating Lady
That's What I'm Going To Do
Drop My Cheating Lady
And Go Find Another Lady
That I Can Screw And Cheat On
Then I'm Going To Drop Her Too

Hey-Lady – Cheat on This
What am I-Saying – You-Already-Did
That's-Why – You're a Cheating-Lady
You'll-Probably – Cheat on The-One
Who-You – Cheated on Me-With

Got to Hand-It to You – Baby
You're a First-Class – Cheating-Lady
What a Crying-Shame
She's to Blame – For-Sure
What-Can-I-Do – I-Think-I-Got-It

(Chorus)
I'm Going To Drop My Cheating Lady
That's What I'm Going To Do
Drop My Cheating Lady
And Go Find Another Lady
That I Can Screw And Cheat On
Then I'm Going To Drop Her Too

Buy Me A Beer (You Bastard) (889.) {Original Version}

Hey – How-You-Doing
That's-Good – That's-Good
No – You-Don't – Know-Me
But-I'm-Broke and Thirsty
Buy-Me a Beer – I'm-Thirsty-Enough
To-Even – Drink-With-You

(Pre-Chorus)
Down On My Luck
Crashed My Truck
Old Lady Left Me
My Pockets Are Empty
I Need
A Freaking-Beer

(Chorus)
Buy Me A Beer
Buy Me A Beer You Bastard
Buy Me A Whiskey
Buy Me A Whiskey You Bastard
Buy Me Another Beer
Before I Puke And Pass Out

Have to Tell-You
You're – All-Right
Long as The-Whiskey's – Pouring
I-Have – No-Worries
'Cause – I'm-Drunk

But – One-Thing
Is-On – My-Mind
If-You – Want-Me
To-Do – Your-Old-Lady
You'll-Have to Buy-Me
A-Bottle – For-Afterwards

(Pre-Chorus)
Down On My Luck
Crashed My Truck
Old Lady Left Me
My Pockets Are Empty
I Need
A Freaking-Beer

(Chorus)
Buy Me A Beer
Buy Me A Beer You Bastard
Buy Me A Whiskey
Buy Me A Whiskey You Bastard
Buy Me Another Beer
Before I Puke And Pass Out

Hey – How-You-Doing
That's-Good – That's-Good
No – You-Don't – Know-Me
I'm-Broke and Thirsty
Buy-Me a Beer – I'm-Thirsty-Enough
To-Even – Drink-With-You

(Pre-Chorus)
Down On My Luck
Crashed My Truck
Old Lady Left Me
My Pockets Are Empty
I Need
A Freaking-Beer

(Chorus)
Buy Me A Beer
Buy Me A Beer You Bastard
Buy Me A Whiskey
Buy Me A Whiskey You Bastard
Buy Me Another Beer
Before I Puke And Pass Out

Buy Me A Beer (You Bastard) (899.1.) {New Version}

How-You-Doing – Bastard
Save-It – I-Don't-Give a Shit
No – You-Don't – Know-Me
But-I'm-Broke and Thirsty
Buy-Me a Beer – I'm-Thirsty-Enough
To-Drink – With a Bastard-Like-You

(Pre-Chorus)
Down On My Luck
Crashed My Fucking Truck
Old Lady Fucking Someone Else
My Pockets Are Empty
I-Need
A-Fucking-Beer

(Chorus)
Buy Me A Beer
Buy Me A Beer You Bastard
Buy Me A Whiskey
Buy Me A Whiskey You Bastard
Buy Me Another Beer
Before I Puke On Your Face

Have to Tell-You
You're-All-Right – For a Sorry-Bastard
Long as The-Whiskey's – Pouring
I-Have – No-Worries
'Cause – I'm-Drunk as Fuck

But – One-Thing
Is-On – My-Mind
If-You – Want-Me
To-Fuck – Your-Old-Lady
You'll-Have to Buy-Me
A-Bottle – For-Afterwards
You-Got-Me – You-Bastard

(Pre-Chorus)
Down On My Luck
Crashed My Fucking Truck
Old Lady Fucking Someone Else
My Pockets Are Empty
I-Need
A-Fucking-Beer

(Chorus)
Buy Me A Beer
Buy Me A Beer You Bastard
Buy Me A Whiskey
Buy Me A Whiskey You Bastard
Buy Me Another Beer
Before I Puke On Your Face

How-You-Doing – Bastard
Save-It – I-Don't-Give a Shit
No – You-Don't – Know-Me
But-I'm-Broke and Thirsty
Buy-Me a Beer – I'm-Thirsty-Enough
To-Drink – With a Bastard-Like-You

(Pre-Chorus)
Down On My Luck
Crashed My Fucking Truck
Old Lady Fucking Someone Else
My Pockets Are Empty
I-Need
A-Fucking-Beer

(Chorus)
Buy Me A Beer
Buy Me A Beer You Bastard
Buy Me A Whiskey
Buy Me A Whiskey You Bastard
Buy Me Another Beer
Before I Puke On Your Face

I'm Dead And Horny (848.)

Baby – You-Look so Fine
What's it Like – Being-Still-Alive
Luscious-Hush – I'm-Not a Freak
I'm-Just a Dead-Man – This-Is so True
That's-Looking to Have a Great-Time
Feeling-The-Living-Warmth of Passion
Inside a Living-Loving-Lady

(Chorus)
Hey Baby – Don't Walk Away
Just 'Cause I'm Dead And Horny
Doesn't Mean My Hard On
Can't Still Be Enjoyed
By Some Fine – Living Lady Like You

Ladies – I'm Dead
Please-Don't – Hold-This-Against-Me
It's-Not-My-Fault – I-Tried to Save-Myself
Struck-Down-By a Fallen – Electric-Cable
Zap – My-Heart-Stopped – I'm a Dead-Man
Walking-Around – With a Permanent – Hard-On

(Chorus)
Hey Baby – Don't Walk Away
Just 'Cause I'm Dead And Horny
Doesn't Mean My Hard On
Can't Still Be Enjoyed
By Some Fine – Living Lady Like You

Hey-Baby – How-About-You
Want to Try a Dead-Man – In-The-Sack
Think-About it Baby – I'm a Dead-Man
Never-Do-I-Get-Tired – Never-Do-I-Have to Stop
I'm-The-Forever – Horny-Dead-Man
Walking-Around – With a Permanent – Hard-On

(Repeat Chorus)

Psycho Lady (998.)

Can-You – Spare a Dollar
Thank-You – I'm-Starving
Give-Me – Five-More
I'll-Tell-You a Tale
About a Psycho-Lady

First – She-Lets-You – Fuck-Her
Second – She-Kills-You-Dead
Third – She-Chops-You to Pieces
Fourth – She-Buries-You – In a Pit

(Chorus)
Psycho Lady – Psycho Lady
She is Fine – She is Hot
Psycho Lady – Psycho Lady
She Always Says Yes
She Never Says No
Psycho Lady – Psycho Lady
If You Fuck Her – You're Dead

Thanks-Man – Don't-Forget
My-Tale – Of a Twisted-Soul
Give-Me – Ten-Dollars-More
I'll-Tell-You – Where-She-Lives

First – She-Lets-You – Fuck-Her
Second – She-Kills-You-Dead
Third – She-Chops-You to Pieces
Fourth – She-Buries-You – In a Pit

(Chorus)
Psycho Lady – Psycho Lady
She is Fine – She is Hot
Psycho Lady – Psycho Lady
She Always Says Yes
She Never Says No
Psycho Lady – Psycho Lady
If You Fuck Her – You're Dead

Screaming Sally {Original Version} (112.)

Poor-Sally – Was-Used – Too-Much
Guys-Would – Pick-Her-Up – Maybe-Feed-Her
Most-Definitely – Got-Their-Good-Time
Sally-Tried-Saying-No – Everybody-Knew-She
Had-No-Control – Such an Easy-Yes
Sally-Would – Never- Admit
This is Actually – What-She-Wanted

Moaning-Sally – Was-Known-As
The-Good-Time-Girl – When-You're-Horny
Go-Pick-Up-Sally – She'll-Let-You
But-One-Night – Sally-Had-Enough
After a Date – Got-Him-Some
Then-Rushed to Put on His-Clothes
When-Sally-Was-Expecting – Some-Cuddling
Guy-Didn't-Even – Want to Kiss-Her-Goodbye

(Chorus)
Screaming Sally – Is Man's Worst Friend
She Hates You – Wants To Eat You
She's A Crazy Hungry – Cannibal Lady
That Always Starts – By Biting Off Your Pecker

Stories-Are-Told of The-Night-When
Moaning-Sally-Became – Screaming-Sally
She-Grabbed – Up a Lamp
Bashed-This-Poor – Fool's-Head-In
Pulled-Down – His-Pants-And
Ate-His-Pecker – Right-Off-Him

Guys-Should-Remember – Sally's-Story
When-They-Go-Out to Find a Quickie
Lady-You're-Lusting – This-Night
Might-Have-Had – Enough of The-Same
Deciding to Follow – Sally's-Lead – Turning
Your-Pecker – Into a Hot-Dog – With-No-Bun

(Repeat Chorus)

Screaming Sally {New Version} (112.1.)

Poor-Sally – Was-Fucked-Too-Much
Guys-Would – Pick-Her-Up – Maybe-Feed-Her
Most-Definitely – They-Got-Their-Lust
Sally-Tried-Saying-No – Everybody-Knew-She
Had-No-Control – Such an Easy-Slut
Sally-Would-Never – Admit
This is Actually – What-She-Wanted

Moaning-Sally – Was-Known-As
The-Good-Time-Piece – When-You're-Horny
Go-Pick-Up-Sally and She'll-Fuck-You
But-One-Night – Sally-Had-Enough
After a Date – Got-Him-Some
Then-Threw-Her – Twenty-Dollars
To-Keep – Her-Mouth-Shut

(Chorus)
Screaming Sally – Is Man's Worst Friend
She Hates You – Wants To Eat You
She's A Crazy Hungry – Cannibal Slut
That Always Starts – By Biting Off Your Dick

Stories-Are-Told of The-Night-When
Moaning-Sally – Became-Screaming-Sally
She-Grabbed – Up a Lamp
Bashed-This-Poor – Bastard's-Head-In
Pulled-Down – His-Pants – And
Ate-His-Dick – While-Ripping-Off – His-Balls

Guys-Should-Remember – Sally's-Story
When-They-Go-Out to Find a Piece of Ass
Lady-You're-Lusting – This-Night
Might-Have-Had – Enough of The-Same
Deciding to Follow – Sally's-Lead – Turning
Your-Dick – Into a Hot-Dog – With-No-Bun

(Repeat Chorus)

Snake Skin Lady Of The Night (812.)

Lonely-Night – Lonely-Pecker
I'm-In-The Need of Evil-Loving
I-Step-Out – Into-The-Darkness
Hoping to Find-Something
That-Will-Change – My-Life

Ladies of The-Night – Wanting-Only
My-Money – Not-One of Them
Wanting to Eat-Me to Death

(Chorus)
Snake Skin Lady Of The Night
She Bites – She Swallows
She's Not For Everybody
Snake Skin Lady Of The Night
One Time With Her Is All You Get
Snake Skin Lady Of The Night
She Bites – She Swallows You Whole
Make Sure You Pay Her – Before You Die

With-White-Fangs and Ruby-Red-Eyes
Snake-Skin-Lady – Hunts-This-Night
Ready to Devour – Bones and All

Snake-Skin-Lady – Sees-Me and Rattles-Her-Tail
She-Sticks-Out Her – Ten-Inch – Forked-Tongue
That-Will-Lick – My-Entire-Body – With-Evil-Love

(Chorus)
Snake Skin Lady Of The Night
She Bites – She Swallows
She's Not For Everybody
Snake Skin Lady Of The Night
One Time With Her Is All You Get
Snake Skin Lady Of The Night
She Bites – She Swallows You Whole
Make Sure You Pay Her – Before You Die

Demon Goat Lady (811.)

Walking-Through – The-Forest of The-Dead
Searching for Demon-Goat-Lady
My-Death-Day is Coming-Soon
Fear in My-Mind – Gives-Me-The-Feeling
That-I-Might – Go to Heaven
When-Hell's – Always-Been-My-Choice

Have to Find-Her – I-Need-Her-Help
Before it's Too-Late – Thank-Hell
There-She is Now – Waving-Me-Over
While-Licking – Her-Sexy – Gray-Lips

(Chorus)
Eat My Soul To Death
Demon Goat Lady
You Are The Finest – You Are The Evilest
Eat My Soul To Death
Demon Goat Lady
Protect My Soul From Heaven
Make Me Burn In Hell Forever

Fine-Looking-Grave-Face – Hair on Her-Ass
Feet of Hoofs – Sharp-Soul-Eating-Teeth
Demon-Goat-Lady is The-Best
When-You're-Feeling – Too-Heavenly

(Chorus)
Eat My Soul To Death
Demon-Goat-Lady
You Are The Finest – You Are The Evilest
Eat My Soul To Death
Demon-Goat-Lady
Protect My Soul From Heaven
Make Me Burn In Hell Forever

Thank-Hell – For-Demon-Goat-Lady
Now-I-Get to Go-To-Hell
Sparing-My-Soul – From-The-Pains of Heaven

I hope you enjoyed Fuckaholic Mind Rockers. Did it piss you off? Did it make you laugh? Did it fuck with your minds? Did it make you want to fuck?

Mind Rockin' has been a wild trip as it prepared me to become something new, something Starblue. My life was stale and sad, Mind Rockin' gave my mind every emotion, from soft to hard. It gave me the freedom to fuck around and also create something that's a mind cleanser. My clogged up mind needed something for my imagination to take control over.

Mind Rockin', I pushed it too the limit, while I had symphonies playing within my mind at the same time. At one point while writing my Mind Rockin' songs, my imagination became so speeding fast, I had to write two Mind Rockin' songs at the same time. I did this just so I could keep up with it. Sometimes my imagination sped so fast, I would write three Mind Rockin' songs at the same time. I'd start on one, move to another and then go back and forth.

Check out my list of Mind Rockin' Songs that are in print on my website. Check out the vast difference from one song to another and only being one number apart. I do not know what or even what's next with Mind Rockin' for myself. So I'm going to put it on a shelf and mentally pick it back up when I feel it's time again to do some Mind Rockin'. Thank you Mind Rocker's, it's been a blast, enjoy the extras.

The Gemini Rising Rockin' Machine

**Most Have Been Renamed
But All Are Bad Songs Now
(Pages 55-83)**

(Side One)
Rocking And Fucking House (73.1)
I'll Be Your Nympho (75.1)
I Remember Rocking And Fucking (906.1)
The Time Is Now (508.1)
It's So Nice To Be Fucked (361.1)

(Side Two)
Fucking (199.1)
I'm Fucking (924.1)
Get High On Fucking (920.1)
Space Clap (20.) (B.S. #20)
Let's Be Friends That Fuck (319.1)

(Side Three)
Fucking And A Rolling (205.1)
Fuck Warrior (877.1)
Thunder Fuck (605.1)
Who's Next (639.1)
Do You Like To Fuck (655.1)

(Side Four)
The Fuck Zone (656.1)
Fuck Bone (679.1)
Fuck Party In Your Panties (830.1)
You're Dead (I Can't Fuck You) (468.1)
Fuck Feast & Fuck Feast (Stained In Blood) (555.1)

Rocking And Fucking House

Work-Week is Over
Fuck it Was a Long-One
Let-The-Weekend – Begin
Start-This – Friday-Night – Up-Right
Time-For-Beer – Rocking and Fucking

(Chorus)
Rock – Fuck
Rocking And Fucking House
Rock – Fuck
It's A Rocking And Fucking House
Rock – Fuck
Rocking And Fucking House
Rock – Fuck
It's A Rocking And Fucking House

Partying-Hearty – Just-Rocking-Away
Jamming – Holding-My-Beer
I-Have a Rocking – Good-Buzz – Going-On
It's-Time to Find a Lady – That-Wants to Fuck

(Repeat Chorus)

She-Sits – On-My-Lap
Gets-Me – Real-Hard – Real-Quick
She-Likes – What-She-Feels
It's-Time to Find a Bedroom
Looking-Forward to Fucking – My-Buzz-Away

(Chorus)
Rock – Fuck
Rocking And Fucking House
Rock – Fuck
It's A Rocking And Fucking House
Rock – Fuck
Rocking And Fucking House
Rock – Fuck
It's A Rocking And Fucking House

I'll Be Your Nympho

Call-Me – If-You-Need – Some-Sex
I'm a Nympho – Horny as Can-Be
I'm-Here – For-Whatever-You-Need
No-Matter – What-The-Challenge
I'm-Here – For-You
I-Can-Do-Anything – Believe-Me

(Chorus)
I'll Be Your Nympho – Yes I'm The One
I'll Be Your Nympho – Yes I'm The One
As Soon As Your Payment Clears
I'll Be Your Nympho

Call-Me – If-You-Need – Some-Sex
I'm a Nympho – Horny as Can-Be
I'm-Just a Phone-Call-Away
Crime – Does-Not-Pay
But-You – Will-Have-To
If-You – Want to Fuck-Me

(Repeat Chorus)

Call-Me – If-You-Need – Some-Sex
I'm a Nympho – Horny as Can-Be
I'm-Out – Fucking-Someone
When-You – Get-No-Answer
Leave a Message
No-Want or Price – Is-Too-Much
On-The-Safe-Side
You-Better-Bring – Extra-Cash

(Chorus)
I'll Be Your Nympho – Yes I'm The One
I'll Be Your Nympho – Yes I'm The One
As Soon As Your Payment Clears
I'll Be Your Nympho

I Remember Rocking And Fucking

Memories of Long-Ago in My-Mind
Calling-Me-Back – Through-Time
To-Forget – All-My-Heavies
To-Party-Hardy and Rock-On
Like-My-Life is On-The-Line

I-Remember
Oh-Yes-I-Do
Summer-Time – Back-Seat-Loving

I-Remember
Oh-Yes-I-Do
Summer-Time – Skinny-Dipping

I-Remember
Oh-Yes-I-Do
Summer-Time – Falling in Lust

And-I-Remember – And-I-Remember
Rocking – And – Fucking

(Chorus)
I Remember Rocking And Fucking
And What It Did For My Soul
I Remember Rocking And Fucking
It Kept Me Young And Free

I Remember Rocking And Fucking
Like A Yesterday's Dream Come True
I Remember Rocking And Fucking
So I'm Going To Start
Rocking And Fucking
'Til The Day I Die

Memories of Long-Ago in My-Mind
Calling-Me-Back – Through-Time
To-Forget – All-My-Heavies
To-Party-Hardy and Rock-On
Like-My-Life is On-The-Line

I-Remember
Oh-Yes-I-Do
Summer-Time – Back-Seat-Loving

I-Remember
Oh-Yes-I-Do
Summer-Time – Skinny-Dipping

I-Remember
Oh-Yes-I-Do
Summer-Time – Falling in Lust

And-I-Remember – And-I-Remember
Rocking – And – Fucking

(Chorus)
I Remember Rocking And Fucking
And What It Did For My Soul
I Remember Rocking And Fucking
It Kept Me Young And Free

I Remember Rocking And Fucking
Like A Yesterday's Dream Come True
I Remember Rocking And Fucking
So I'm Going To Start
Rocking And Fucking
'Til The Day I Die

The Time Is Now

Oh-Baby – I-Need-You
You-Got-It – Going-On
Let-Me – Tell-You-Baby
I-Want-You so Sexy-Having-Bad

If-You-Want a Man
That-Knows – How to Thrill
All-You – Gotta-Do
Is-Let – Your-Hair-Down
And-Take-Off – Your-Pants

(Chorus)
The Time Is Now
Let's Go Somewhere And Fuck
The Time Is Now
Let Your Lips Say Yes – Just Like Your Mind Does
The Time Is Now
Let's Go Somewhere And Fuck All Night Long

Oh-Baby – Don't-Be-Shy
You're so Fine and Fuckable
Grab – Your-Things-Baby
Follow – My-Love-Bone

I'm-Taking-You
Home-Sweet-Home
So-You-Can – Get to Know
Me and My – Bed-Better
And of Course – My-Love-Bone

(Chorus)
The Time Is Now
Let's Go Somewhere And Fuck
The Time Is Now
Let Your Lips Say Yes – Just Like Your Mind Does
The Time Is Now
Let's Go Somewhere And Fuck All Night Long

Oh-Baby – I-Need-You
You-Got-It – Going-On
Let-Me – Tell-You-Baby
I-Want-You so Sexy-Having-Bad

Oh-Baby – Don't be Shy
You're so Fine and Fuckable
Grab-Your-Things-Baby
Follow – My-Love-Bone

(Chorus)
The Time Is Now
Let's Go Somewhere And Fuck
The Time Is Now
Let Your Lips Say Yes – Just Like Your Mind Does
The Time Is Now
Let's Go Somewhere And Fuck All Night Long

Welcome – Come on In
Where – Magic – Happens
Every-Single – Sweet-Night
My-Place is The-Place
Fucking so Fine
Happens – All-The-Time

(Chorus)
The Time Is Now
Let's Go Somewhere And Fuck
The Time Is Now
Let Your Lips Say Yes – Just Like Your Mind Does
The Time Is Now
Let's Go Somewhere And Fuck All Night Long

It's So Nice To Be Fucked

(Chorus)
It's So Nice To Be Fucked
I Tell Ya
It's So Nice To Be Fucked
You Know It
It's So Nice To Be Fucked
Come On Everybody
It's So Nice To Be Fucked

It's so Very-Sad to Me
That-Everybody – Now-Seems
Not to Want to Fuck
They're so Down
Into – Their-Lives

It's-Just
Speeding-Away so Fast
When-They – Finally-Have
The-Time to Fuck
There's – No-One-Around
For-Them to Fuck

(Chorus)
It's So Nice To Be Fucked
I Tell Ya
It's So Nice To Be Fucked
You Know It
It's So Nice To Be Fucked
Come On Everybody
It's So Nice To Be Fucked

I-Don't-Have – The-Best-Life
A-Lot of Times
It's-One-Big – Old-Bummer
But-I-Never – Let-Life
Bring-Me-Down – Too-Far
Because – I-Have
A-Lot of Fucking
Inside – My-Soul
To-Keep-Me – Going-On

So-When-Life
Starts-To – Bring-Me-Down
I-Grab a Hold of My-Love
And-Give-Her a Great-Big-Fucking

(Chorus)
It's So Nice To Be Fucked
I Tell Ya
It's So Nice To Be Fucked
You Know It
It's So Nice To Be Fucked
Come On Everybody
It's So Nice To Be Fucked

If-You-Ever – Want to Know
How-Great – Fucking-Can-Be
Give-Me a Call – I'll-Let-You-Watch-Me

'Til-Then – Try-To – Do-Your-Best
To-Bring-Some-Fucking – Into-Your-Life

(Chorus)
It's So Nice To Be Fucked
I Tell Ya
It's So Nice To Be Fucked
You Know It
It's So Nice To Be Fucked
Come On Everybody
It's So Nice To Be Fucked

Fucking

Fucking is Happiness
Happiness is Fucking
Fucking is Sadness
Sadness is Fucking
Fucking is Togetherness
Togetherness is Fucking
Fucking is Loneliness
Loneliness is Fucking

Fucking is Everything and Everything is Fucking
Come-On-World – Repeat-This-With-Me

(Chorus)
Fucking – Is What We Have
Fucking – Is Our Way Of Life
Fucking – Keeps Us Strong
Fucking – Keeps Us True
Fucking – Will Save The World

Fucking is Happiness
Happiness is Fucking
Fucking is Sadness
Sadness is Fucking
Fucking is Togetherness
Togetherness is Fucking
Fucking is Loneliness
Loneliness is Fucking

Fucking is Everything and Everything is Fucking
Come-On-World – Repeat-This-With-Me

(Chorus)
Fucking – Is What We Have
Fucking – Is Our Way Of Life
Fucking – Keeps Us Strong
Fucking – Keeps Us True
Fucking – Will Save The World

I'm Fucking

No-Fucking – Last-Year
No-Fucking – Last-Month
No-Fucking – Yesterday
However-Today – I'm-Fucking

Just-Like-That – I'm-Fucking
Pretty-Lady – Kissed-My-Lips
Pretty-Lady – Kissed-My-Love-Bone
Now-Today – I'm-Fucking

(Chorus)
I'm-Fucking – Can't You See
I'm-Fucking – Can't You Tell
I'm-Fucking – Hooray For Me
I'm Fucking World
It Feels So Good To Be Fucking
I Wish You Could Be Fucking Too

No-Fucking – Last-Year
No-Fucking – Last-Month
No-Fucking – Yesterday
However-Today – I'm-Fucking

Just-Like-That – I'm-Fucking
Pretty-Lady – Kissed-My-Lips
Pretty-Lady – Kissed-My-Love-Bone
Now-Today – I'm-Fucking

(Chorus)
I'm-Fucking – Can't You See
I'm-Fucking – Can't You Tell
I'm-Fucking – Hooray For Me
I'm Fucking World
It Feels So Good To Be Fucking
I Wish You Could Be Fucking Too

Get High On Fucking

I-Was in Love – She-Cheated on Me
I-Fell in Love-Again – She-Cheated on Me-Too
I-Fell in Love – Once-Again
She-Cheated on Me – With-My-Best-Friend

Boo to You-World – Boo to You-Love
I'm a Great-Fucker – I-Deserve-Better
I'm so Down – What-Can-I-Do
To-Get-Myself – Out of This – Love-Funk

(Chorus)
I'm Going To – I'm Going To
Get High On Fucking
That's What I'm Going to Do
Fuck You World – What's Your Problem
If You Won't Help Me
I'm Going To – I'm Going To
Get High On Fucking – All By Myself

I-Was in Love – She-Cheated on Me
I-Fell in Love-Again – She-Cheated on Me-Too
I-Fell in Love – Once-Again
She-Cheated on Me – With-My-Best-Friend

Boo to You-World – Boo to You-Love
I'm a Great-Fucker – I-Deserve-Better
I'm so Down – What-Can-I-Do
To-Get-Myself – Out of This – Love-Funk

(Chorus)
I'm Going To – I'm Going To
Get High On Fucking
That's What I'm Going to Do
Fuck You World – What's Your Problem
If You Won't Help Me
I'm Going To – I'm Going To
Get High On Fucking – All By Myself

Space Clap (B.S. #20)

What-The-Fuck is That
I-Can't-Believe – What-I-See
Glowing and Hovering – In-The-Air
It's- A – U-F – Fucking-O
Don't-Want to Be – Anal-Probed

Should-I-Run – For-My-Life
Should-I – Wave-Hello
Light – Shines-Down
Up-In-The-Sky – I-Go
Entering – The-Belly of The-Ship

(Chorus)
What The Fuck
Am I Going To Do
Now That I Got
A Bad Case Of Space Clap
No Doctors On Earth
Can Save My Dick
From My Bad Case Of Space Clap

It's-Dark – Can't-See a Thing
Red-Arrow – Pointing-The-Way
I-Walk – The-Distance
That-Leads-To a Giant-Clear-Door

Though – The-Clear-Door
Can't-Believe – What-I-See
Beautiful – Three-Breasted
Space-Ladies – Everywhere
Let an Earth and Space
Fuck-Fest – Begin

(Chorus)
What The Fuck
Am I Going To Do
Now That I Got
A Bad Case Of Space Clap
No Doctors On Earth
Can Save My Dick
From My Bad Case Of Space Clap

Space-Ladies – In-Different-Colors
Purple – Pink – Orange and Even-Blue
I-Love-This – Here's to Hoping
That-The-Shades – Match-The-Carpet

Handed a Glass – I-Down-It
Handed a Pipe – I-Toke-It
Sexy-Space-Ladies – Like to Party
Yes-Yes – Take-Off-Your-Clothes
Three-At a Time – Works-For-Me

(Chorus)
What The Fuck
Am I Going To Do
Now That I Got
A Bad Case Of Space Clap
No Doctors On Earth
Can Save My Dick
From My Bad Case Of Space Clap

Space-Ladies
Amazingly – Long-Tongues
I'm-Drunk – I'm-Stoned
I-Keep-Going – I'm so Horny
Start-And-Finish – Move-Along

I-Have – No-Time to Waste
Twenty-More – Space-Ladies
In-Waiting to Enjoy – My-Manhood
What a Perfect – Night

Dropped-Off – Right-Before-Dawn
I'm-Spent – My-Dick is Numb
Going-Home – Sleep to Dusk
Where's – My-Car

(Chorus)
What The Fuck
Am I Going To Do
Now That I Got
A Bad Case Of Space Clap
No Doctors On Earth
Can Save My Dick
From My Bad Case Of Space Clap

Sun-Shining – Though-My-Window
Slept a Whole-Day
Can't-Move – I'm-Spent
Damn – I-Have to Take a Piss

Oh-Fuck – Oh-Fuck
It-Burns – It-Burns so Bad
My-Dick is Colored-Rainbow
Can't-Stop – My-Painful-Pissing
Going to Pass-Out – Please-No-More

What – Was-I-Thinking
Just-One-Rubber – Could-Have-Prevented
Me-From-Catching – The-First-Case
Of-Space-Clap – On-Earth
Why-Me – Why-Me

(Chorus)
What The Fuck
Am I Going To Do
Now That I Got
A Bad Case Of Space Clap
No Doctors On Earth
Can Save My Dick
From My Bad Case Of Space Clap

Let's Be Friends That Fuck

My-Friend – Calls-Me
Another-Lover – Has-Left-Her
She's-Crying-The – I'm-All-Alone
Come-Over and Talk to Me
Because – I-Need-You

I-Have to Be – Her-Rock
That-She-Can – Lean-On
Agreeing to Let – My-Shirt-Get-Wet
From-All-The-Tears – She'll-Be-Crying

(Chorus)
Let's Be Friends That Fuck
I'm Still Alone
Now You Are Again
So Dry Your Eyes
I Have A Great Idea
Let's Be Friends That Fuck

My-Pretty-Friend – I've-Known – For-Years
Looks at Me so Surprised – I'm-Standing
Above-Her – With-My-Hand-Out
She-Closes – Her-Mouth and Smiles
Then-She-Gives-Me – Her-Hand

We-Look – Each-Other in The-Eyes
Saying-Yes – To a Night of Fucking
Both of Us-Shaking – Wanting to Say-No
But-Our-Loneliness – Is so Heavy
We-Bite-Our-Tongues and Let-Ourselves-Go

(Chorus)
Let's Be Friends That Fuck
I'm Still Alone
Now You Are Again
So Dry Your Eyes
I Have A Great Idea
Let's Be Friends That Fuck

The-Silence – That-Came-After
Was-Not – That-Heavy – After-All
As-We-Put – Our-Clothes-Back-On
Staring-Silently – Then-Laughing
As-We-Talked at The-Same-Time
Both of Us-Saying – The-Same-Thing

(Chorus)
Let's Be Friends That Fuck
I'm Still Alone
Now You Are Again
So Dry Your Eyes
I Have A Great Idea
Let's Be Friends That Fuck

We-Are-Happy – Doing-Great
Finding a Release – That-We – Both-Needed
We are Not in Love and Not-Trying to Be
Both of Us-Know – That-Love-Sucks
And-What-We-Have - is - Something-Very-Special

Being-Friends – That-Fuck
Is-Wild and Very-Different
Especially – When-Our – Fucking-Friend
Has a Date – With-Another
That-The-Other – Doesn't-Want – Them to Have
Getting-Embarrassed – When-Reminded
This-Thing – We-Have is Not-Love
It's – Just – Fucking

(Chorus)
Let's Be Friends That Fuck
I'm Still Alone
Now You Are Again
So Dry Your Eyes
I Have A Great Idea
Let's Be Friends That Fuck

Fucking And A Rolling

Wow – What a Lady
Can't-Keep – My-Eyes-Off-Her
She-Looks so Lovely
She-Has – Such a Pretty-Face
With a Body – Built-For-Thrills

I'm so Drawn to Her
Have to Take – My-Shot
Can't-Let – The-Chance of
Perfect – Fucking
Slip-Away – From-My-Pecker

(Chorus)
Fucking And A Rolling
Moaning And Groaning
Come On Baby Let's Go For It
I Want To Have So much Fun
Fucking You – All Night Long

She' so Perfect – She's so Sweet
With-Such a Lovely-Voice – Talking to Me
Watching as Her – Cheeks-Blush
From-Knowing – What-I-Want

(Chorus)
Fucking And A Rolling
Moaning And Groaning
Come On Baby Let's Go For It
I Want To Have So much Fun
Fucking You – All Night Long

My-Place – Your-Place
Come on Baby – No-Better-Time
I-Know – I-Got-What-You-Need
To-Make-You – Explode

(Repeat Chorus)

Fuck Warrior

Been-There – Fuck-That
I-Don't – Even-Have-To
Take-Off – My-Pants
To-Get-It – Real-Quick

Don't-Believe-Me – Well-Then
Let's-Have a Fuck-War
Begging-Will – Only-Make-Me
Make-You – Moan-Even-Louder

(Chorus)
I'm A Fuck Warrior – Baby
That Has Just Sexually Conquered You
Good Luck With Walking The Same
Can You Even Remember Your Name
Better Hurry And Retreat – Baby
'Cause I'm A Fuck Warrior
That Never Fires A Pre-Warning Shot

I-Get-So-Much – Fine-Ass
I've-Ran – Out-Of-Room
I-Have to Come-Over to Your-House
Mark-My-Victory – On-Your-Bed-Post

Don't-Believe-Me – Well-Then
Let's-Have a Fuck-War
Begging – Will-Only-Make-Me
Make-You – Moan-Even-Louder

(Chorus)
I'm A Fuck Warrior – Baby
That Has Just Sexually Conquered You
Good Luck With Walking The Same
Can You Even Remember Your Name
Better Hurry And Retreat – Baby
'Cause I'm A Fuck Warrior
That Never Fires A Pre-Warning Shot

Thunder Fuck

Thunder-Fuck – Super-Ready
I-Take-This-Hot – Fucking-Night
With-My-Giant – Thunder-Love
Searching-For – The-Right-Ones
That-Loves – Some-Fine-Fucking

I'm-The-One – Yes-I-Am
That-Can – Take-You-Higher
To-The-Height of Your-Desire
If-You-Want – This-Fucking of Mine
All-You-Gotta-Do – Is-Join-In

(Chorus)
Thunder Fucking / Across The Sky
Great Looking Bodies On Fire
That Lustfully Burn With Desire
When They're In Thunder Fucking Motion
So Come On Baby – Let's Thunder Fuck
Let's Thunder Fuck – Until You Pass Out

Where-You-Going – Thunder-Fucking-Lady
I'm-Only-Half-Way-Through – Don't-Leave
These-Three-Ladies – All-Alone
Trying to Cope – With-My-Thunder-Fucking

That's-Okay – Take-Your-Moment
I-Understand – Completely-Baby
Believe-Me – I-Know-That-My
Thunder-Fucking is Intense – And-The-Reason
You-Never – Want to Leave

(Chorus)
Thunder Fucking / Across The Sky
Great Looking Bodies On Fire
That Lustfully Burn With Desire
When They're In Thunder Fucking Motion
So Come On Baby – Let's Thunder Fuck
Let's Thunder Fuck – Until You Pass Out

Who's Next

Fuck-Party – Fifty-Couples-Strong
Freedom-Reigns – When-Fucking
Flows-Free – With-Many
Different-Partners – In-One-Night

There is No-Shame – For-Any of Us
We-Are-Not – Doing-Anything-Wrong
It's-Our-Bodies – It's-Our-Life
We-Have The Right – To-Fuck-Swing

(Chorus)
Who's Next – I've Just Enjoyed Myself
And I'd Like To Do It Again
So – Who's Next
I'm Ready For Some More
Of Whatever You Got
So Come On Baby – Be My Next Fuck

Be-Almost-Polite – While-You're
Enjoying-Yourself – Fucking-Another
That-Is-Not – Your-Lover
By-Remembering – That-They're
Someone's-Lover as Well

Enjoy-Yourself – Very-Much
Help-Them – Do the Same
It-Might-Be – Their-First-Time
They're-Nervous – They're-Turned-On
It's-Up to You to Show-Them
What-Free-Fucking – Is-All-About

(Chorus)
Who's Next – I've Just Enjoyed Myself
And I'd Like To Do It Again
So – Who's Next
I'm Ready For Some More
Of Whatever You Got
So Come On Baby – Be My Next Fuck

Do You Like To Fuck

I-See-You-Once – I-See-You-Twice
You-Shake – Your-Ass
Like-You – Want-Me to Want-It
So-Very – Sexy-Bad

I-Try to Catch-Up to You
Your-Shake – Is so Fast
It-Slows – Me-Down
Watching – What-I-Want – As-I
Watch-Your – Fine-Ass
Getting-Further – Away-From-Me

(Chorus)
I Catch My Breath
Say To You – Baby
Do You Like To Fuck
'Cause I'd Like To Fuck You
With My Rock Hard –Thunder-Fuck

You-Stop – Your-Shaking
Turning-Around to Check-Out
The-Man – Who-Thinks
He-Has-It in Him to Make-You
Slow – Down – Enough
Making-Your-Shaking – Turn to Lust

In-Your-Eyes – I-Can-Tell
That-I-Have to Be – As-Quick-As
Your-Very-Fine – Shake
To-Allow-Me – My-Chance-To
Fuck-You as Only-I-Can

(Chorus)
I Catch My Breath
Say To You – Baby
Do You Like To Fuck
'Cause I'd Like To Fuck You
With My Rock Hard –Thunder-Fuck

The Fuck Zone

Feel – My-Heartbeat
Look-Into – My-Eyes
I-Lust-You-Baby – Let's-Get it On

I'm-More – Than-Ready
To-Start-Up-My – Fuck-Engine
For-Your – Loving-Pleasures
That-Will-Last – All-Night-Long

(Chorus)
Baby It's Time To Enter
The Fuck Zone
Don't Worry About Self Control
Leave Ever Thing To Me
Because Baby When I'm In
The Fuck Zone
I Don't Stop 'Til Dawn

Good-Morning – You're-Welcome
I-Feel-Great – Today
You're-Just – What-I-Wanted
I'm-Glad-I-Have – What-You-Needed

Now-That-Our – Fuck-Zone is Over
Baby it's Time – For-Me to Say – Goodbye
Don't-Cry – Don't-Get-Mad
I-Don't-Mind – Coming-Back-Tonight
It-Gives-Me-Pleasure – Helping-Out a Fine
Lady-Like-You – Out of Your – Fuck-Rut

(Chorus)
Baby It's Time To Enter
The Fuck Zone
Don't Worry About Self Control
Leave Ever Thing To Me
Because Baby When I'm In
The Fuck Zone
I Don't Stop 'Til Dawn

Fuck Bone

Fucking on My-Mind
Fuck-Bone in My-Pants
I'm-Doing-Fine – Tonight
Let's-Dance-Baby – Let's-Dance
Let-Me – Turn-You-On

Yeah-Baby – It's-All-Real
When-We-Get – All-Alone
I'll-Show-You – My-Fuck-Bone
Love-It-Baby – I'll-Even-Let-You-Feel-It
I'm-That-Kinda – Amazing

(Chorus)
Thank Your Body Baby
For Your Great Time
You're So Welcome
I Know You Love – My Fuck Bone
But Baby – My Fuck Bone
Will Never Be Satisfied
With Only One Love Slice

I'm a Hard-Bad-Man – That-Can-Go
I'll-Make-You so Happy
Then-I'll – Make-You so Sad
When-I-Put – My-Fuck-Bone
Back – In-My-Pants
Welcome to The-Way-It-Is
Where-I-Come – Then-I-Go

(Chorus)
Thank Your Body Baby
For Your Great Time
You're So Welcome
I Know You Love – My Fuck Bone
But Baby – My Fuck Bone
Will Never Be Satisfied
With Only One Love Slice

Fuck Party In Your Panties

We-Went-Out-Once – Fucked-Twice
What a Night – I'll-Never-Forget
Time-Goes-By – I've-Forgotten-Your-Name
Out of The-Corner of My-Eye
I-See-Your – Body and Face
Standing-There – Ready to Be-Enjoyed
What-Else-Can-I-Do – But-Come-Up to You
Look-You – In-Your-Eyes – And-Say

(Chorus)
Baby I've Heard – Baby I've Heard
There's A Fuck Party In Your Panties – Tonight
Hope I'm The Only One – Invited
'Cause You Know – How I Hate To Share
What's In Your Panties – 'Til I'm Done

You-Slap-My-Face – I'm so Cruel
Out of The-Blue – I-Was-Rude
Giving-No-Thought – About-Your-Feelings
And-The-Man – Who-Shares-Your-Life
What-Can-I-Say-Baby – What-Can-I-Do
I'm a Man – That-Likes to Get-It-On
So-Let-Me-Repeat – Myself-To-You

(Chorus)
Baby I've Heard – Baby I've Heard
There's A Fuck Party In Your Panties – Tonight
Hope I'm The Only One – Invited
'Cause You Know – How I Hate To Share
What's In Your Panties – 'Til I'm Done

Baby-If-This-Makes – You-Feel-Better
Your-Man – Can-Have-You-Back – When-I'm-Done
After-Twice-More – Times-With-You
Fine-Once in My-Life – Before-You-Walk-Away
What-Else-Can-I-Do – But-Look at You
And-Say – One-More-Time
(Repeat Chorus)

You're Dead (I Can't Fuck You)

In-My-Life
I've-Met and Fucked
A-Whole-Lot of Different-Ladies
I've-Had – My-Troubles
Plenty of Sorrows – But
Life-Goes-On so Does-Fucking

One-Day – I-Was-Enjoying-Myself
Getting to Know –Someone
Pretty-Soft – Warm and New
Out of The-Corner of Your
Dead-Eyes – You-See-Me

(Chorus)
You Come From A Nightmare
Stinking To Low Hell
Saying To Me – I Love You
Telling Me – You're My One
Telling Me – You Want Me To Fuck You
In Deep Shock I Reply
You're Dead – I Can't Fuck You

You-Looked-Like – Cold-Death
Wrapped in Something – That-Use to Be-Alive
As-You-Grabbed-My-Date – Off-My-Lap
And-Ate-Her-Face – Like it Was a Raw-Warm-Ham
You-Licked-Your-Lips – I-Took-The-Hell-Off
Saying-Dead-Lady – You're-Not-Eating-Me

(Chorus)
You Come From A Nightmare
Stinking To Low Hell
Saying To Me – I Love You
Telling Me – You're My One
Telling Me – You Want Me To Fuck You
In Deep Shock I Reply
You're Dead – I Can't Fuck You

With-Pieces of My-Date
Stuck – Between-Your-Teeth
You-Chase – After-Me-Pleading
That-You-Want – My-Loving
That-You'll be My-Loving-Dead-Lady
If-I – Fuck-You – Just-Once

For a Dead-Woman – You-Sure-Are
Fast on Your – Dead-Feet
Noticing-This as I-Run-Faster
While-You – Shorten-Your-Distance

(Chorus)
You Come From A Nightmare
Stinking To Low Hell
Saying To Me – I Love You
Telling Me – You're My One
Telling Me – You Want Me To Fuck You
In Deep Shock I Reply
You're Dead – I Can't Fuck You

Picking-Up – My-Speed
Turning-Fast – Around a Corner
You-Come – Around-Faster
Wanting-Me – Wanting-My-Love
All-You-Get-Instead – Is-Your-Head
Knocked-Off – By a Jagged-Board
That-I-Found – Laying on The Ground
I-Guess-You're-Not – Being-Fucked-Tonight
Very-Dead-Now – Dead-Lady

(Chorus)
You Come From A Nightmare
Stinking To Low Hell
Saying To Me – I Love You
Telling Me – You're My One
Telling Me – You Want Me To Fuck You
In Deep Shock I Reply
You're Dead – I Can't Fuck You

Fuck Feast & Fuck Feast (Stained In Blood)

Spin-The-Bottle – Key-Parties – Game of Smiles
Midnight-Quickies – In-The-Wet-Night
Love-Is-In-The-Air so Is-The-Smell of Fucking
Been a Long – Time-Coming
For-This-Fuck-Feast to Take-Off
Its-Clothes – And-Get to Moaning and Groaning

Sex-Appetites – Are-Quenched
Sharing-That – Someone-Special
Panties-Being – Given-Away
Bras-Thrown – Into-The-Bonfire
People-That-Don't – Know-The-Other
Having-Fucking – Fun-Together

(Chorus)
Fuck Feast – Tonight All Night
Bring Your Manhood
Bring Your Womanhood
And Get To Fucking

Whiskey and Lipstick – Candles and Oils
Two-Ladies for One-Man – Two-Men for One-Lady
There is No-Wrong or Right
This-Is a Fuck Feast
For-The – Totally-Free
That-Like to Smile – With-Their-Clothes-Off

If-You-Can't – Get-It-Up
It's-Okay to Just-Watch
That's-Part of The-Fuck-Feast-Rules
But it Can't-Compare to Joining-In
Having a Great – Fuck-Feast-Time

(Chorus)
Fuck Feast – Tonight All Night
Bring Your Manhood
Bring Your Womanhood
And Get To Fucking

(Turns Into: Lust Feast – Stained in Blood)

Lust in The-Air – Brings-Out a Murderer
A-Being so Twisted – That-He'd-Rather-Kill
Than-Have-Sex – Fuck-Feast-Style
Monster – Came-Out of The-Woods
Started-Shooting – Naked-Fuck
Feast-People to Their-Bloody-Deaths

Their-Embrace – Became-Their-Last
As-This-Murdering – Monster
Kept-Firing-Away – With a Smile
The-Body-Count is Piling-Up
Because-He-Has so Many-Bullets

(Chorus)
Fuck Feast – Stained In Blood
One Gun Wielding Lunatic
And A Whole Bunch Of Naked
Fuck Feast – Dying People

Mister-Murder is In-Ecstasy
The-Dirty-Bastard – Dirtying-His-Shorts
Rapid-Fire – Killing-Death
He-Won't-Stop-Shooting – Until
He-Runs-Out of Bullets

Faces-Ripped-Apart – Hearts-Stop-Beating
Tits and Dicks – On-The-Ground
All-This-Could – Have-Been-Stopped
By-Keeping – Guns-Away
From-Lunatics and Keeping
Fuck-Feast-People – Free and Protected
While-They – Fuck-Feast-Around

(Chorus)
Fuck Feast – Stained In Blood
One Gun Wielding Lunatic
And A Whole Bunch Of Naked
Fuck Feast – Dying People

**{Other Mind Rockin' Books by
The Gemini Rising Rockin' Machine.}**

Book One: Who Am I?

Book Two: Mind Rockin'

Book Three: Big Time Love
Book Four: Love High

Book Five: Siphon Your Minds

Book Six: Do You Remember Rock And Roll
Book Seven: Rock And Roll Bachelor

Book Eight: The End

Sunshine Dealer Meets Thunder Love

Watch The Pig People Eating Dog Apple Pie

The Gemini Angelic Demon Dance

Triple Play Of Love, Sadness And Sexy Lust

Double Play Of Humanity's Disharmony

Book Zero: The 2.0 Versions Of
Who Am I? & Mind Rockin'

Purgatory's Full: The Musical

{Other Non- Mind Rockin' Book}

Purgatory's Full: A Song, A Dream Or A
Cold Hard Reality In Thirty-Six Parts

Vote For Me Anyway
(Written on **10/25/2014** – Election Day was on my mind.)

Yes – I-Have-Passion – In-My-Blood
Lust in My-Large – Heart
With a Strong-Desire – In-My-Mind
For-This-Other – Woman
Which-I-Have-Slept-With – 111 Times

But it's Not – My-Fault
For-She – Seduced-Me
With-Her-Wild – Wicked-Evil-Ways
She's a Temptress – I-Tell-You
That-Tempted-Me – When-I-Was at a Lowest

I-Let-Myself-Go – Not-Knowing
I-Was-Being-Seduced by Evil-Lust
She's a Succubus and I-Was-Her
Helpless – Love-Slave

But-Now-Thankfully to My-Lord
My-Wife – Family-Friends and
All of You – I am Myself – Once-Again
Free-From-That – Hell-Cat's
Evil – Seductive – Tempting-Ways

I-Have-Fallen – That is True
But-Now – I-Have-Risen – Above-Evil
Stronger – Prouder – More-Full of Faith
I-Can-Look-Everyone in Their-Eyes
Right-Now and Say – That if You-Vote-For-Me
You-Have-Voted – For a Changed-Man

And-You – Never-Know
The-Other – Guy
Might-Be a Bigger-Sinner
That-Does it With-Animals
Know – What-I'm-Saying

Touch The Screen
(Written **10/26/2014** – This person can be trusted)

Welcome – All-Thy-Faithful
Welcome – Those-That-Dabble – With-Sin
Welcome – All-That-Live-With-Sin – Inside-Themselves
Sin is Around-Us – Tempting-Us at All-Times
I-Know-About-Evil – I-Can-Spot-It
Just-Like a Moth – To a Flame

I-Can-Say to All-Those-Here
That-Sin is Here – Today-With-Us
It's-In-Every-One of You
Waiting to Come-Out and Play
The-Only-One – That's-Free-From-Sin
Is-I – Your-Savior
From-My – God-Touched-Soul
I-Forgive-All of You – For-Your-Sins

But-The-Strain – I-Feel so Deeply
For-Being – Your-Strong-Savior
Leaves-Me – Tired and Weak
Making-Me-Need – Your-Help
If-You-Want-My-Soul to Keep-On-Soaring
High in The-Sky – Next to God
Then-I-Need to Be-Compensated

Your-Money – All-That-You-Can-Afford
Can-Make-That-Happen – My-Fellow-God-Lovers
The-More-Generous – You-Are
The-More-Time – I-Can-Stay-Next to God
So-Don't-Give to Me – Give-For-Yourself
Because-God and I – Love-You

And to All-Those – Watching on Television
I-Want-You to Touch-The-Screen
Feel-My-Love and My-Faith
Now-Call – Right-Now
Send-Me – All-The-Money – You-Can
God-Bless-Me – God-Bless-You

The Perfect Pill (610.)
(Written: **09/30/2014**)

(Spoken)
One-Day – You're-Soaring and Scoring
Your-Love-Life is Something to Brag-About
Then-One-Night – You're-Saying to Someone
This-Has-Never – Happen to Me-Before
Their-Smile – Turns to a Frown
Then-They-Got to Be-Going – Leaving-You-All-Alone
Wondering and Worrying – You-Turn on The-TV
There's a Man-Talking-About – What-Happen to Him
Just-Like – What-Happen to You
And-All-He-Had to Do – Was-Say-Yes
To-Me – The-Perfect-Pill
I-Will-Help-You – When-Your-Down
By-Making-You – Get-Back-Up

(Sung)
Life's so Great – When-Your-Getting-Some
Making-Love – At-The-Drop of Your-Clothes
But-Life – Is a Journey
Sometimes-You-Need a Little-Help
From a Pill – Just-Like-Me

I'm-The – Perfect-Pill
To-Help – You-Out
When-Your – Over-The-Hill
And-Can't-Make – Your-Way-Back-Up
Just-Swallow – Me-Down
Perk-Yourself – Back-Up
Cause-Life is Too-Short
Not to Have – Some-Fun
Including – Getting-You-Some

(Spoken)
What-Are-You-Waiting-For? – Call-Right-Now
Operators-Are-Ready and Able to Help-You
With-Your – Small-Problem

Untitled Sex Story #1 (Pages 88-93)

7:33 on a Friday night. "I'm bored Rachel."

"So am I Dean."

"What do you want to do?"

"I don't know."

"Well Rachel let's think of something. We're tired of fucking each other. I know I could use some fresh."

"That's just what every woman wants to hear her lover tell her on a Friday night Dean."

"I know, ain't I great?"

"That's debatable."

"You want to smoke a joint?"

"Yes, roll a thick one."

"As thick as my dick?"

"No, I want to get stoned not just a little buzzed."

"You're a riot tonight Rachel."

"Stop yapping and start rolling."

"No need I have one rolled to go."

"Well fire it up already."

Dean fires up the joint and tokes away then hands it to Rachel, "Love you Rachel."

Rachel takes the joint, "Love you Dean."

Thirty minutes later Dean and Rachel are kissing while playing with their favorite parts of the other. Rachel is just about to tell Dean to head to the bedroom when the phone rings. "I hope it's Sally," Rachel says as she pushes Dean off her and jumps up from the couch.

"Damn, I was ready to go."

"Me too but it's Sally. Let's hope the orgy is back on."

"Damn straight. I'm in the mood for lots and lots of..."

"Shut up, I'm answering," Rachel says as she walks away to talk with Sally.

"Where are you going? I want to hear what's going on."

Rachel pays no attention and keeps on walking. Three minutes later she walks back to Dean, "Great news Dean, I have three men waiting for me at Sally's house that want to fuck me."

"Well great fucking for you Rachel but what about me?"

"How should I know?"

"You didn't ask Sally for me who's there for me to fuck?"

"No, why should I?"

"Because I'm your boyfriend."

"What's that got to do with it?"

"Let me think..... a lot."

"Don't worry Baby, I'm just busting your big balls."

"That's one of my favorite things about you Baby. Damn ain't our lives great?"

"Very great. Now who should I let fuck me first?"

"What about me?"

"I'll let you fuck me tomorrow."

"No, I mean who am I going to be fucking tonight?"

"Well there's always Sally."

"I hope there's better than her at the orgy."

"What's wrong with Sally? She's fine."

"I know but I'm in the mood for someone new."

"Well great news Baby. As soon as we get there, we will be the twentieth couple. So you have twenty women to choose from tonight."

"Damn. Alright, that's what I'm talking about. I wonder how many couples there tonight that it'll be their first time."

"Probably a few."

"What's the rules? It ain't one on one until you finish is it?"

"I didn't ask, but I hope not."

"I know what you mean. I like it better when you can stay or leave whenever you want to. It makes it easier to have two women at the same time."

"You're right about that. Well, two men for me."

"Let's go then."

"No, I want to freshen up and get redressed."

"Why? You look fine and sexy."

"I know and thank you. I just want every man there to look at me and want to fuck me. I also want every woman there to be jealous when they look at me."

"I can understand that. Damn Rachel you're the greatest."

"I know Dean and right back at you."

"I love it that you understand and approve the fact that I need to fuck more than just one woman."

"I love that about you too Baby. I tell you, at that orgy we met and fucked at two years ago, it was like love at first sight for us. Wasn't it Dean?"

"Yes it was Rachel. You were so great, I only wanted sex with you all night long."

"Yeah, my boyfriend was so pissed at you when you took me away from him that night."

"Same with my girlfriend. I think she's still pissed at you."

"Screw 'em, they weren't worth keeping."

One hour later Dean and Rachel arrive at Sally's house. "Look at all the cars Dean."

"I know. It's going to be hard finding a parking spot."

"Well hurry up, I'm looking too fine to be waiting."

"There's one and it's all mine."

Dean parks and turns off his car. "You know what I'm going to do Rachel?"

"What's that?"

"I'm going to do my favorite thing that I like to do tonight."

"What's that Dean?"

"I'm going to walk up to a new couple that's standing together. You know the kind of couple that's too afraid to get things started."

"What are you going to do after you walk up to them?"

"I'm going to walk up to the woman and kiss her right in front of her man. Then I'm going to walk her away from him and go fuck her brains out."

"That sounds like fun, I guess?"

"It is. Remember that's how I met and fucked you."

"That's right. I'd been to a orgy before but it was the first time for my boyfriend."

"Hopefully tonight the man will do the same thing your boyfriend did."

"What's that?"

"Like you don't remember Rachel?"

"Remind me Dean."

"Your boyfriend stood there with his mouth hanging open wide as he watched me give you the fucking of your life."

"That was great," Rachel responds as she laughs lightly.

Dean and Rachel get out of Dean's car and start walking towards Sally's back door. "I'll see you at the end of the night Rachel."

"See you then." They stop at the door and Dean waits to knock until he gives Rachel a kiss goodbye for the night. "You look so fuckable Rachel."

"So do you Dean. Happy fucking."

"Happy fucking to you too."

After knocking, the door opens up and Sally says hello and
kisses both her friends. Dean does what he told Rachel he
wanted to do. After that he walks off and finds someone
else new to fuck with. Rachel has men standing in line to
fuck her so to say. She lets two men have her at the same
time then she walks off to find someone more special.
Fast forward and six hours later Dean and Rachel meet up
with the other and both of them look happy and sad at the
same time. "Hello Rachel."

"Hello Dean."

"Did you have a great time?"

"Yes. How about you?"

"I had a great time. Rachel there's something I need to tell
you. I met..."

"I need to tell you something as well Dean."

"Okay but me first. I met someone Rachel. Someone that
I want to start dating in between orgies."

"I'm happy for you Dean."

"You are Rachel? Why?"

"Because I've done the same thing."

"That's great. It's been nice fucking you Rachel, so long."

"It's been great fucking you too Dean So long and keep in
touch. Maybe we'll fuck again someday."

"That's sounds great Rachel."

Untitled Sex Story #2 (Pages 94-99)

"Hello, I'm single and I'm free tonight."

"Well good for you!"

"Come on Baby, you haven't even seen me with my clothes off."

"Good, I don't think I'm missing much."

"Is that right?"

"Yes, that's right."

"Well Baby stop looking at my face and look between my legs."

"I don't think so, please go away."

"Okay, no problem. It's just...."

"It's just what?"

"Well tomorrow, I'm taking a cruise and I have an extra ticket I'd like to give to someone hot and sexy, that wants to spend a week out on the ocean getting to know me."

"Why didn't you say so... That's me."

"It is?"

"Yes, I love the ocean."

"Me too but do you like to fuck?"

"No, I like to make love."

"That's a shame, I'm into fucking. I guess this is where we say goodbye."

"Wait a minute... Damn, okay, you can fuck me as long as you take me with you on your cruise."

"That won't do."

"What won't do?"

"Me fucking you."

"I don't understand what you mean?"

"I fuck you, you fuck me, we fuck together."

"I can do that."

"But do you want to?"

"Yes I do?"

"I don't know... I got it. Let's fuck tonight before our cruise tomorrow. That way I know you're serious about fucking."

"I don't know... Okay take me to your home."

"No yours."

"Okay, follow me, my apartment is only three blocks away."

"Lead on sexy."

"What is your name?"

"Do you really want to know it Sexy Lady?"

"No not really Sexy Man."

"Sexy Lady, I'm easy to please."

"Well, I'm not, Sexy Man."

"No problem Sexy Lady, I have a big dick."

"That's good to know, Sexy Man."

Ten minutes later, Sexy Man and Sexy Lady are fucking their brains out.

"I just love your tits and ass, Sexy Lady."

"I know, aren't they great? Now shut up Sexy Man and give me more."

"I can do that."

Twenty minutes later, Sexy Man and Sexy Lady are through fucking. Sexy Man gets up to take a piss after he lets Sexy Lady go first. When he gets back Sexy Lady has a question for him.

"Where are they?"

"Where are what?"

"Don't play dumb, where are the tickets for the cruise?"

"Sorry Sexy Lady, I lied. I have no tickets for a cruise. Do you want to go grab something to eat?"

"No I don't want to go grab something to eat... I want cruise tickets and I want them right now... I don't care if you have to pull them out of your ass to get them."

"Sorry Sexy Lady, all I have up my ass is crap."

"That's so funny... Let me get this straight... You lied to me just so you could fuck me."

"Yes."

"Why would you do this? How could you do this to me?"

"Don't be hard on yourself Sexy Lady, I do this all the time."

"You're a sorry bastard."

"I can live with that. It's been great Sexy Lady but I've got to be going."

"Have someone else to get to so you can fuck them?"

"Yes I do, I'm so lucky, I fuck all the time. I just love my life."

"Yeah your life is great Sexy Man... There's only one problem?"

"What's that Sexy Lady?"

"Me."

"You?"

"Yes me you sorry bastard. You owe me and you owe me big."

"I don't think so. What you needed I gave to you already."

"You owe me Sexy Man because you made me cheat on my boyfriend."

"No I didn't, you did that all by yourself."

"But you tricked me into cheating on my boyfriend."

"No I didn't. Sexy lady you forgot all about your boyfriend in hopes of going on a cruise with me. Tell me something, was I better than your boyfriend at fucking you?"

"Yes, you sorry bastard."

"I understand."

"You understand what?"

"If I leave you, your sex life will be boring."

"I wouldn't say boring."

"Does your boyfriend wait until you get yours before he gets his?"

"Yes... Sometimes... No he doesn't."

"Tell you what Sexy Lady, why don't you drop him for the next couple of days and come with me?"

"Where would we go?"

"Does it matter?"

"No it doesn't. Give me a few minutes and I'll pack a bag."

"Make sure you pack all sexy clothes."

"No shit. What did you think I would pack, baggy pants and big sweaters?"

"Not for one moment, Sexy Lady."

"Sexy Man, let me get this straight, all we're going to do is fuck each other?"

"Yes Sexy Lady and maybe after I fucked you enough times I might just fall in love with you."

"Well I'll cross my fingers, Sexy Man."

"That might help, Sexy Lady."

Sexy Man and Sexy lady, share a laugh and then they fuck one more time before they take off to fuck some more for the next few days.

Bags packed and the door open for Sexy Man and Sexy Lady to leave and in their way stands trouble, in the form of Sexy Lady's boyfriend.

"What the Hell is going on here?"

"I don't want to hear it Boyfriend, we're through. Now get out of our way."

"No, I will not. You're my woman and I will not let you get away from me."

"Sexy Man would you fight my boyfriend to keep me?'"

"Yes I would, Sexy Lady."

"Good. Boyfriend would you fight my Sexy Man to keep me all to yourself?"

"Yes I would."

"Good. Then let's all three of us head to the roof. Don't either of you ask any questions just get walking."

Three minutes later Sexy Man and Boyfriend are fighting like two wild dogs. They keep fighting until they get close enough to the edge of the roof to satisfy Sexy Lady.

Sexy Lady with all her might pushes both Sexy Man and Boyfriend off the roof to their falling deaths.

'That's much better. Both of them were nothing but sorry bastards, I won't miss either of them. World I have to ask you this, what does a sexy and beautiful lady like me have to do to find the right man?'

**Blake and Barbara (John) (Extended Website Version)
(Pages 100-112)**

What Blake planned to say but did not have a chance to
was – "Hello, I notice that you are alone and so am I.
You've heard this, I've said this before. But beep it, I'm
lonely and you're fine, so sweet looking lady what do you
say? Would you like to make love with me after I buy you
the three D'S – Drinks, Dinner, and Dessert, whatever you
want or whatever it will take for you to say yes to me. So I
can take my time and enjoy every sweet and sexy curve
you have that a man like me just lusts after."

However this is what happened when Blake said, "Hello, I."
"Sit down. Never mind. This is not what I ordered, so walk
away, then come back to me and do it right this time."

Blake thinks, what the sexy love is going on? This is weird
but then again it is very hot. I think this lady is either a
swinger or she thinks she paid for me to come up to her
and give her the night she always wanted. Love it, I would
kick my ass if I ruined this great sexy night without giving it
my very best. Think I'll say this.

"Pardon me beautiful. I am a replacement for you. I'll add
this, a much better replacement. Here let me sit down so I
can give you my full attention. Beautiful sexy lady, I was
just told to come here and give you what you paid for. But
due to someone stupid, your original date, he took the
information sheet with him so for right now I can only
guess what you want me to do for and to you. If I
understand correctly you paid for the deluxe package. Is
that correct?"

"Yes I did," says the confused, sexy lady that is not sure if
she is happy about this turn of changes that has been
brought to her.

Blake notices this, he steadies himself so his words to this
hot sexy lady will remain calm and sexy confident.

"Um sorry I didn't even get your name." "Barbara." "I like that, Beautiful sexy Barbara. Oh what I am going to do for you, Beautiful sexy Barbara. You're so fine I would almost do for you what you want from me for free. But like you know, bills are a bitch and my talented body is all I have to survive with and pay them damn bills."

"Yes, very well my replacement for the night. The great thing for myself is the fact that I can only guess what that is like for you. I have no problems, well maybe just one, you."

Blake does not hesitate in saying. "Great thing, I am a problem solver that has so many love tools at my beck and call, that any problem can be forgone in a matter of only a few sex having moments."

"Well that sounds very hot and satisfying. What is your name anyway?"

"What do you want my name to be sexy Barbara?"

Barbara blushes and says, "I don't know." Then she jokingly says, "How about Mr. Big?"

Blake smiles knowing that he has Barbara right where he wants her at the same time he is trying to suppress his excitement because this is the greatest pre-sex thing that has ever happened to him. "Tell you what Beautiful sexy Barbara, just call me Animal."

"Animal? I think not you bad, bad man. I'll just call you God, like that is what you better make me say over and over again if you know what I mean?"

Blake is very turned on when he says, "No that won't do. Barbara you will have to call me God-God because I am twice the special that you can't help but fall in loving love with."

Barbara looks at this man in front of her and shakes her head slightly in disbelief. "That was thick."

"So am I Barbara."

"John, I'm going to call you John for now. John you have turned me on like I have not been in a very long time. Please whatever you do, do not be all about bragging with me and when you get me all alone you are just like everybody else. Give me a little then get yours before I am even half way there. You see I am divorced, couple of years now, I've had my dates and boyfriends but in the end they all turned out the same. Wanting to be my soon to be lazy man that gives it to me like they and only they want to, which pisses me off John. Like I have no say in it, don't get me started..." Barbara pauses

"You see John, I'm single, I'm rich, and you better make me moan. Sorry John that Ex of mine still pisses me off so much. I mean look at me I'm hot and he takes off with some young slut that wants to live free in the forest like they did a long time ago. I hope the bastard runs out of food and the only thing around for him to eat are bugs and tree bark."

"Shut up."

"Excuse me!"

"Barbara I said shut up. I am on the clock, I am here to turn you on, not to hear you bitch. So that's a penalty."

"A penalty John!"

"Yes Barbara, so I want you to stand up, come over to me, sit on my lap and give me a kiss like we are the only ones in this entire room."

Barbara feels the excitement of this moment inside her making her want to let it last a little while longer.

Barbara puts her right hand up to her head and runs it through her hair, like she's letting John know that she is thinking about it very sexily seriously. Then Barbara pulls her right hand away from her hair and shakes her head no, which she follows up by saying. "I will not John."

Blake sits back in his chair and smiles a sexy smile to Barbara, enjoying what he is about to say. "If you don't Barbara I'll leave you sitting here wanting to be made to feel like a real woman."

"John, please, I can't. I would be so embarrassed."

"Barbara do you know anyone here? Do you come here often?"

"No never."

"Then what do you care what anyone thinks? As far as they are concerned we might just be a couple in love, or a couple that has had a fight and right here in public we make up like the in love couple we are."

Blake sits forward half way in his chair and looks Barbara right into her sexy eyes. "You only live once Barbara, sit there and do without or get up and get you some like the woman who is so sure of herself that she is willing to pay someone what she could get for free. Well that is not completely true Barbara, you will never have anyone better than me unless of course you pay for me again."

Barbara gasps almost quietly with a pretty face that is flushed from this man's show of sexual dominance over her. Barbara inhales deeply making her large breasts heave causing her shirt to stretch tighter against them. Barbara keeps doing this until she makes Blake open his mouth as far as he can without him falling out of his chair.

Barbara lets out her breath hard enough to make Blake's

Love-Bone jerk around in his pants. Blake sits there holding his breath, hoping she keeps this hot sexual moment going on. Barbara looks into Blake's eyes and very slowly straightens her stretched out shirt. When Barbara is through with her sexy straightening, she then places both of her hands on top of the table and begins to tap her ruby red fingernails against it.

Without warning she stops tapping and says to a startled Blake, "John, no one, I mean no one has ever talked to me like that. And I like it. You better be all that you say."

"That and even more my sweet, Beautiful, sexy Barbara."

Blake pauses to say yes to himself out of sexual happiness then he continues on. "Barbara If you want this night to proceed with you purring and moaning, all you have to do is what I say and I'll make you think and feel like the sun rises and sets in my pants."

Barbara says to herself, damn this man sure talks a great sexual game, let's see if he can play it as sexually great. "Alright John, you are in control. I'll give myself to you, but please don't break me. I'm very fragile right now."

"Then you are very lucky Barbara because that is my specialty. Now 1-2-3 come to me my love pet, let me make you feel like you are in Heaven."

Barbara's eyes are shining like stars, as her heart is pounding in her chest. She wonders if John can hear her heartbeat as she sits on his lap, giving him the kiss he demanded from her. Two people that are hot and turned on are not caring who's watching them kiss like two lust starved lovers.

They continue kissing with a abundance of passion showing as footsteps come walking towards their table. Mr. Waiter stops at John and Barbara's table and stares for a few seconds getting turned on before he begins to speak

to them of restaurant protocols, the forever do's and don'ts.
"Please, please we cannot have that here. This is a
respectable, first class restaurant."

Blake pulls his lips away from a not wanting him to do so
Barbara and says, "Well then shut up and bring us your
best bottle of champagne and don't forget this fine lady is
going to be paying for everything."

Barbara gets off of John's lap slowly, nicely turned on and
embarrassed, the waiter looks jealously at his table guests
then walks away doing what he was commanded to do.
Dinner is served, it is eaten between light sexual dinner
conversation. Twenty minutes later dinner is over, John
stands up as Barbara signs for the check, leaving the
waiter that wants to be John a fifty dollar tip as a
consolation prize.

Barbara and her John, pardon me. Barbara and John walk
out of the restaurant together arm in arm with her leaning
her head on his shoulder. Once out and on the sidewalk
the valet walks up to them and says to them, "Miss
Bridgesong, I'll be right back with your car and Mister?"

"Stiffboard. John Stiffboard."

"Mr. Stiffboard, I'll be right back with your car as soon as I
get Miss Bridgesong's first."

"That's okay Tony, Mr. Stiffboard will be riding with me, he
will be back much later to pick his car back up. That is not
a problem, is it Tony?"

"No, no problem at all Miss Bridgesong, I'll be right back."

Tony hurries away wishing he was Mr. Stiffboard when all
of a sudden with the repeating of Mr. Stiffboard in his mind
he gets it, the joke. Mr. Stiffboard is the funniest name
Tony as ever heard anyone ever come up with or happen
to own.

Tony stops laughing and says out loud not very loudly, 'Lucky bastard, what I would not give to have my chance with Miss Bridgesong. I would give it so much better to her than that impostor of love.'

Blake and Barbara are standing there silently still arm in arm when Blake looks over at Barbara and asks her. "Am I driving?"

"No way John, my car's my baby, the first very big thing that I bought for myself after my divorce." Barbara takes her arm away from Blake's, she takes a few steps away from him and then turns back around facing him to look him straight into his eyes. Blake looks back at Barbara knowing that he is just about to receive some information about her past.

"I drove my new baby to my ex-husband's new house right out of the dealership's show room. I sat there in his driveway revving my baby up fully, really nice, loud and long. That silly cheating bastard came out of the safety of his new house, like what is going on, who is that? He walked up to my baby all nervous and mad looking. I rolled down the window, took off my sunglasses, then I flicked him off..." Barbara pauses to laugh.

"He was about to say something to me when I told him to save it. Then I had the great time telling him that my new baby gave me more pleasure when I revved it up than his small pecker ever did for me while he fumbled around like a fool trying to make love to me."

Blake looks at Barbara not knowing what to say when he can't help himself anymore. The temptation is too great for him to hold back his laughter anymore and he just lets it all out. Blake is laughing with tears coming out of his eyes as Barbara's eyes start to glaze over with a certain amount of rage in them.

"How dare you laugh at me like this John? Or should I say

my ex-john. You just made a very big mistake and I want my money back all $1,000 dollars of it."

Blake gulps thinking to himself, 'Hell yeah, I'm getting a grand to make Barbara purr, wait a minute he re-thinks, no I'm not.'

When Barbara's eyes stop him cold from thinking and laughing, Blake straightens himself up, takes another couple of seconds and says to Barbara. "Hang on sexy Barbara, I'm not laughing at you, I'm laughing with you."

"Well John I am not laughing and I am pissed off right now. So sad for you, I'm going home alone."

Barbara starts walking away slowly. Blake says nice job to himself, then he collects himself by telling himself that he's got this. "I understand, I will not try to stop you Barbara, it's just..." Blake stops talking giving Barbara her chance to change things back around.

Barbara turns back around and stands there with both of her hands on her hips, looking at Blake like tell me it's just what. Blake knows this but does not blink or lick his lips. While at the same time wanting very much so to chew on those sexy looking hips, that right then started to sway slowly in anticipation of Blake finishing what he was going to say.

"Okay John, I am tired of waiting for you to finish, so I guess I have to ask you this, It's just What?"

Blake blinks his green eyes at Barbara's blue eyes a few times. "It's just... What you said and how you said it, well you were very funny Barbara. I did not mean to upset you, it's just..."

"'Oh no you don't John, you better answer me if you want your chance at making money while enjoying my so hot and lonely wanting to be touched sexy body."

"Wow Barbara you just made me hard and ready to go"

"Did I?"

"Yes you did, take a look for yourself."

"I will not."

"Yes you will, look and feast your eyes on what your sexy words made happen in a quick sexy moment."

Barbara lets her hands fall away from her hips as she begins to tap her right foot on the sidewalk five times before she stops and says. "Damn you John, I'm mad."

"No you are not Barbara, you are just nervously turned on, letting your mind have its chance to make this stop before it goes any further. Now take a look." Barbara sighs and looks up at the starlit night sky until the count of ten then she takes her sight away from the night sky directly to John's crotch.

Two almost strangers stand about seven feet away from each other as they hear a car coming towards them. Before Tony brings Barbara's car to a halt, the wind all of a sudden blows hard like a warning that a storm is on its away. The car comes to a complete stop as the wind blows even harder, making the driver's door slam back shut when Tony opens it to get out.

"It's just what John?" Barbara quickly yells out to Blake.

"It's just when you said that I felt like I was finally meeting the real you, and I like her."

Barbara smiles and blushes at the same time, while nodding her head yes. "Okay John you can come with me to the hotel where I rented a room for the night for us. And when we get there John all I want you to do is please me."

"That is what you paid for and what I am looking so forward to doing."

"Then let's go John, time is wasting." Right then just like it started the wind dies down to a calm gentle breeze.

Fast forward twenty three minutes as they arrive at their sexual location for the night, right after Barbara scares the shit out of Blake with her very fast driving first. Nine minutes later Barbara is lying on the bed naked with her dress and panties hanging off the bottom left side of it.

Blake is telling her how sexy her body is as he walks around the bed so he can see her body from all its different sides. While Blake is doing this he is slowly taking off his clothes until he is as naked as Barbara. Two people that want each other stare at each other with the look of full lust in their eyes.

Barbara sighs as John lays on the bed and gives her a few light kisses on her lips. Blake then takes the tip of his tongue and slightly licks so softly and sexy the right side of Barbara's neck. Barbara moans as Blake takes the tip of his tongue away from Barbara's neck and places it ever so tenderly on her right shoulder.

Sixty nine breaths later Blake leads the tip of his tongue to Barbara's right big beautiful looking breast and then he stops licking her breast and looks up her and asks her this. "Are you ready my sexy beautiful Barbara for me to make you feel like every dollar you spent has been totally sexy worth it?"

"Yes John take your time and please me ever so fine."

I know this is a bad time to cut into this story right when it is just about to get so ever lusting good. But I did tell you on my website that I would make a note in the story when the full sexual encounter was about to happen so nobody would miss it. Are you ready? Here it goes, count it off with me Mind Rockers. 1-2-3. The Full Sexual Encounter has started and now it has ended. Let's take a pause together for a moment for I am sexually spent, how about you?

Two lovers lay down beside each other panting in rhythm from their two hours of love making. Blake pulled no kisses as he made sure to give Barbara everything she always wanted. All is well and fine as Blake starts to think too much about doing the right thing. "Barbara my name is Blake and I am not who you think I am."

"You're not?"

"No I am not. I am just a lonely man that came up to you for a chance of having a great time. I am not the man you ordered or even the man that took his place."

"What!? This can not be? You bastard! What kind of man are you, to do this to me? I hope you had your fun because I am going to destroy you."

Barbara gets up from the bed very fast and angrily grabs her panties and dress off the floor. She takes no time at all to be dressed and walking towards her purse.

Blake knows instantly that he made a very big mistake, it just took him until now to find the right words to say, "Barbara please wait a minute. At first yes, my only intention was to use you for a great time but now Barbara, I love you."

"Love me!? Love me!? I don't even know who you are. I can't believe this, I feel sick, I think I should go to the hospital."

"Now wait a minute Barbara, it's not like I have a disease or something. To be honest, you are not so innocent Barbara. You did after all pay someone to make love to you or should I say to have sex with you."

"That is true, I paid for one of them and you are not one of them." Barbara stops talking long enough to enjoy the pain that is in Blake's eyes before she continues on. "Blake you're just normal, not special. I just knew it, deep down I knew something was going on, you were good but not great."

"Well I know my ears are ringing from your loud lustful moaning in them. You were really loud, deny it all you want, I know you enjoyed me lots while I just had a good time."

"Well Blake let's see how good of a time you have when I call the cops and tell them how you took advantage of me all for money. I'll tell them I was weak and all that. How does that sound to you Blake? Does that sound Jake to you? Ha, ha, ha."

"Sounds like a bunch of shit to me, you Witch."

"Say you're sorry or I'll call right now!"

"I'm Sorry! You."

"You what?"

"You very pretty lady."

"That's better, maybe I have a use for you after all. Okay this is the way it is going to be. You come when I call you. Give me your phone."

"Why?"

"Do not ask questions just do as I say always."

Barbara reads Blake's number off to herself so she can load it up on her phone. "Do I get to have your number as well?"

"No you do not, I call you, you do not call me. Now where was I? Oh yes that's right. Blake look at me and understand very well what I tell you. You don't ever tell anyone about you and I and maybe just maybe, I'll let you be my love toy. Just nod your head yes."

Blake nods his head. "That's a good love pet, now get the Hell out of here I'm done with you for now."

"How do I get back to my car?"

"Walk, it will do you some good and also it will give you time to clear your mind to the idea that you now belong to me to do as I please with."

Blake leaves with his head hanging low. While Barbara thinks to herself, 'Men are so easy and dumb. Am I in love or lust?"

Demon Goat Whore (811.1) (Hidden Bonus)

Walking-Through – The-Forest of The-Dead
Searching for Demon-Goat-Whore
My-Death-Day is Coming-Soon
Fear in My-Mind – Gives-Me-The-Feeling
That-I-Might – Go to Heaven
When-Hell's – Always-Been-My-Choice

Have to Find-Her – I-Need-Her-Help
Before it's Too-Late – Thank-Hell
There-She is Now – Waving-Me-Over
While-Licking – Her-Sexy – Gray-Lips

(Chorus)
Eat My Soul To Death
Demon Goat Whore
You Are The Finest – You Are The Evilest
Eat My Soul To Death
Demon Goat Whore
Protect My Soul From Heaven
Make Me Burn In Hell Forever

Fine-Looking-Grave-Face – Hair on Her-Ass
Feet of Hoofs – Sharp-Soul-Eating-Teeth
Demon-Goat-Lady is The-Best
When-You're-Feeling – Too-Heavenly

(Chorus)
Eat My Soul To Death
Demon Goat Whore
You Are The Finest – You Are The Evilest
Eat My Soul To Death
Demon Goat Whore
Protect My Soul From Heaven
Make Me Burn In Hell Forever

Thank-Hell – For-Demon-Goat-Whore
Now-I-Get to Go-To-Hell
Sparing-My-Soul – From-The-Pains of Heaven

Mind Rockers, on 12/06/2017, I wrote 'Let's Say Fuck It' as my one thousandth and one Mind Rockin' song. Two days before this I wrote my one thousandth Mind Rockin' song 'We Could Say Fuck It'. I was going to stop there then the thought came to me, if I ever wrote another Mind Rockin' song what would it be? To get rid of this thought forever I wrote 'Let's Say Fuck It', then moved on. On 08/15/2018 for a personal reason, I wrote my one thousandth and two Mind Rockin' song. So at this time I've decided that I will no longer number any more of the new Mind Rockin' songs I decide to write.

After a thousand and two, numbers no longer matter. In truth, they haven't mattered since I reached five hundred. Like I said, I was going to stop but why should I? Mind Rockin' is fun and a way to stimulate my mind. So no more numbers just free Mind Rockin' from now on. If I was sad, this would make me happy. However, I'm not sad. I'm not happy all the way I want to be but hopefully before too long I will be. Freedom to be able to release a book like Fuckaholic brings me this much closer to the happiness I want.

 A lot will think I'm fucked up for releasing Fuckaholic and they are free to do so. Hopefully a lot will also say fuck it and buy this book and discover what freedom is all about. Fuckaholic is my freedom, what is yours? Both sides, the Left and the Right are pulling at us like we can't be ripped apart. Hate is so Fucking easy. It's a lot Fucking easier than Love. It's also a lot Fucking easier than liking some thing as well.

Government needs the people and the people need the Government. Is this the truth? As of right now and before this time, the answer is a big YES. What of tomorrow? Will freedom even exist? Not if Government gets bigger.

Fear the man always and never trust them. In truth they need us more than we need them. Sadly Government is the only thing holding this world together. This is not the people's fault, there is no other way. Fuck That! I say this to you world, Fucking is better than Death. Bombs of Death are not sexy. I know they turn me off. Lack of freedom turns me off as well. For without freedom, Fuckaholic would never exist. Love or hate this book, that's up to you. I just wonder who will be the first one that says fuck it and contacts me to be the first one to add music to one or more of these Mind Rockin' songs.

The time is now to really say fuck it before we can't say fuck it. Why? Because neither the Left or the Right wants us to. How dare us to want this much freedom? What good does this do for either of them? The answer is very simple, Nothing. They can't do anything with nothing and nothing pisses them off more than this. Am I a sitting duck? Am I fish in a barrel? Am I just too fucked up to be of any concern? Time will tell all. Until then I want to have some fun. Freedom = Fuckaholic – Fuckaholic = Freedom. Fun? Comes right in the middle of them.

The first one that contacts me and is for real, gets first, second, third pick. Maybe all picks. That is up to you and just how much you want to be able to sing Fuck in so many different ways, in so many different songs. What song would I like to be picked first? Lunch Fuck. Here's a reminder why. Baby – I'm-Horny-Hungry / All-The-Sexy-Time / I-Have-My – Breakfast-Fuck / I-Have-My – Dinner-Fuck .... Baby-What-I-Need – From-You / Oh-So-Much – Is-For-You / To-Be-My – Lunch-Fuck.

Just how much would you like be able to sing these, my lyrics on stage, in front of a crowd that sings these lyrics back to you? If only I could sing good, I would sing these lyrics myself. I can't but you Fucking can, so let's make a lot of Fucking money and show the world what Fuckaholic Freedom is all about. One more thing, I'm not Satan or a Demon, nor do I believe that I am. Take care of yourselves Mind Rockers and find some Fuckaholic Freedom for yourselves. Enjoy my four new unnumbered Mind Rockin' songs, that start on the very next page.

Lick Shit (09/08/2018)

Do-You – Have
Total-Hate – In-Your-Heart
Do-You – Hate-The-World
And-All-Its – Moving-Parts
That's-Fucked-Up

Do-You – Like-Wars
That-Never – End
Do-You – Hate-Peace
For-All of Humanity

(Chorus)
Then Why Don't You Lick Shit
Why Don't You Lick All Kinds
Of Different Shit – All Day Long
You Can Also Take A Bite
Or Ten If You Want To
You Shit Licking Hater Of Everything

Do-You – Want a World
That's-Full of Killers
Do-You – Like-The-Idea of
Predators and Prey
That's – Fucked-Up

Do-You – Want
The-World to End
So-You and Your-Own
Can be The-Only to Survive

(Chorus)
Then Why Don't You Lick Shit
Why Don't You Lick All Kinds
Of Different Shit – All Day Long
You Can Also Take A Bite
Or Ten If You Want To
You Shit Licking Hater Of Everything

Mother Earth Is The Fucking Boss (09/08/2018)

Drill-Deeply – Inside-Her
So-You-Can – Open-Her-Up-Wide
Blow-Her to Pieces
With so Many-Bombs

She-Feels-This – Deeply-Inside-Herself
And-She – Doesn't-Like-It
Mother-Earth – Has-Had-About-Enough
And-She – Ain't-Going to Take-It-Anymore

(Chorus)
Listen Up Real Close
Mother Earth Is The Fucking Boss
Don't Believe This
Then Ask All Those That Came Before Us
That's Right You Can't
And Why Can't You – Because
Mother Earth Is The Fucking Boss
She Doesn't Have To Fucking Answer
The Next In Line That's To Become Extinct

Live – For-The-Day
Stop – All-The-Wars
Stop-Scarring – Mother-Earth
Stop-Trying to Kill-Us-All

Take a Deep-Breath
While-You-Stop – And-Think
Listen to Your-Conscious
That's if You-Have-One

Warnings – Are-All-Around
Stop-And-Think – Pay-Attention
Before-It's too Fucking-Late
If-You-Need a Reminder – Well-Then

(Repeat Chorus)

Rock, Fuck, Death And Roll (09/08/2018)

Sleep-All-Day so The-Spider
Can-Lay – Her-Nest
Deeply-Inside – Your-Mouth
Wake-Up-Early – All-Miserable
But-Safe – Just so You-Can
Punch-That – Time-Clock

The-Work-Week is Long
The-World is Too-Overbearing
And-Fucking – And-Death
Are-The-Hottest – Things-Going-Today
And-What-The-Fuck – Are-You-Going to Do-About-It

(Chorus)
If You Ask Me – I Think It's Time To
Rock, Fuck, Death And Roll
All Night Fucking Long
It's Time To Rock, Fuck, Death And Roll
Just Like The Rest Of The World Does
Every Single Fucking Day

Half-Eaten – Sandwich
Might-Look so Delicious to You
While-It's – Laying-In a Pool of Blood
Just-Don't-Pick it Up – And-Eat-It
Because – It's-Tainted by Death
And it Will-Taste – Very-Bad

Damn – Everything's-Fucked-Up
And-What-The-Fuck – Are-You-Going to Do-About-It

(Chorus)
If You Ask Me – I Think It's Time To
Rock, Fuck, Death And Roll
All Night Fucking Long
It's Time To Rock, Fuck, Death And Roll
Just Like The Rest Of The World Does
Every Single Fucking Day

If You Fuck A Demon (You Will Burn In Hell)
(09/08/2018)

Those-That-Like to Fuck
Listen to This – Fucked-Up-Shit
Some-Time-Ago – Some-People
Got-Together and Conjured-Up a Demon
So-They-All – Could-Fuck-it

Do-I-Have to Tell-You
How-Bad of An-Idea – This-Was
These-Dumb-Fucks – Really-Fucked-Up
When-They – Tried to Fuck
Something-That's – Engulfed in Hell's-Fire

(Chorus)
Warning To All Fuckers
That Wants To Fuck A Demon
If You Fuck A Demon – You Will Die
If You Fuck A Demon – You Will Burn In Hell
And Yes – You Will Fucking Burn Forever

Just-Say-No to Fucking-Demons
Just-Say-No to Burning in Hell
Maybe-You – Should-Try-Some
Human-Fucking – First
Who-Knows – You-Might-Like-It

Human-Fucking – Isn't-Always-Safe
But at Least – You-Won't-Have to
Conjure-Up a Demon – From-Hell
For-You to Fuck – For-The-Night

(Chorus)
Warning To All Fuckers
That Wants To Fuck A Demon
If You Fuck A Demon – You Will Die
If You Fuck A Demon – You Will Burn In Hell
And Yes – You Will Fucking Burn Forever

**The Original Six Bad Song Mini
Basted on Songs... Written during the late 80's
(Pages 121-126)**

Fuck Them Faster (31.) **(B)**

Wacker (37.) **(B.)**

Fuckers (39.) **(B.)**

Fight And Fuck (56.) **(B.)**

Wood Job (69.) **(B.)**

It's My 120th Song So Fuck You (120.) **(B.)**

Fuck Them Faster (31.) (B)

All-Right – Everybody
This-Is a Bad-Song
If-You-Can't – Take-Fuck
Stop-Singing – Right-Now

Because – I-Fuck-Them-Faster
And-I-Fucking – Love-It
And-They-Fucking – Do as Well
Just-Fucking – Ask-Them
When-They-Take a Break
From-Fucking – Faster

(Chorus)
Come On Everybody
Let's Fuck Them Faster
Hurry Up – Get Your Fucking Over With
Then Find Another Luster
And Fuck Them Even Faster
Hurry Up – Get Your Fucking Over With
Then Find Another Luster
And Fuck Them Even Fucking Faster

All-Right – Everybody
This-Is a Bad-Song
If-You-Can't – Take-Fuck
Stop-Singing – Right-Now

Because – I-Fuck-Them-Faster
And-I-Fucking – Love-It
And-They-Fucking-Do as Well
Just-Fucking – Ask-Them
When-They-Take a Break
From-Fucking – Faster

(Repeat Chorus)

Wacker (37.) (B.)

Ladies – Are-Fine
Ladies – Are-Great
But-Ladies – Are-Not
As-Fast – As-Ready
As-My – Left-Hand

So-After-I – Get-Turned-On
I-Run-Home & Wack-Off
You-Know-Why – Because

(Chorus)
I'm A Wacker – I Wack Off In The Morning
I'm A Wacker – I Wack Off In The Afternoon
I'm A Wacker – I Wack Off In The Evening
I'm A Wacker – I Wack Off Before A Date
I'm A Wacker – I Wack During A Date
I'm A Wacker – I Wack Off After A Date

Ladies – Are-Fine
Ladies – Are-Great
But-Ladies – Are-Not
As-Fast – As-Ready
As-My – Left-Hand

So-After-I – Get-Turned-On
I-Run-Home & Wack-Off
You-Know-Why – Because

(Chorus)
I'm A Wacker – I Wack Off In The Morning
I'm A Wacker – I Wack Off In The Afternoon
I'm A Wacker – I Wack Off In The Evening
I'm A Wacker – I Wack Off Before A Date
I'm A Wacker – I Wack During A Date
I'm A Wacker – I Wack Off After A Date

Fuckers (39.) (B.)

Good-Morning – Babe
How-You-Doing – Today
How-Would – You-Like
To-Fuck – This-Morning

You-Want – On-Top
You-Want-Me – On-Top
Anyway-You-Want to Fuck-Babe
I'm-Up & Ready – For-Anything

(Chorus)
Fuckers – We-Are
She – Don't-Mind
You Know I Don't Mind
Fuckers – We-Are
We Fuck When We Say Hello
We Fuck When We Say Goodbye
We Also Fuck Just To Be Fucking

Good-Night – Babe
How-Was-Your – Long-Day
How-Would – You-Like
To-Fuck – This-Evening

You-Want – On-Top
You-Want-Me – On-Top
Anyway-You-Want to Fuck-Babe
I'm-Up & Ready – For-Anything

(Chorus)
Fuckers – We-Are
She – Don't-Mind
You Know I Don't Mind
Fuckers – We-Are
We Fuck When We Say Hello
We Fuck When We Say Goodbye
We Also Fuck Just To Be Fucking

Fight And Fuck (56.) (B.)

I-Try-Real-Hard to Be a Nice-Guy
But-I-Can't – Help-It
I-Like to Fight-And-Fuck

There's-Always a Dumb-Bastard
That-Runs-His – Punk-Ass-Mouth
And-After – I-Beat-Him-Down
I-Feel-Like – I-Could-Use a Fuck
So-Here's – My-Song

(Chorus)
I Like To Fight And Fuck
I'll Whip Your Punk Ass
Then I'll Find A Woman To Fuck
I Like To Fight And Fuck
I'll Whip Your Punk Ass
Then I Might Even Fuck Your Woman
If She's Fuckable – That is

I-Try-Real-Hard to Be a Nice-Guy
But-I-Can't – Help-It
I-Like to Fight-And-Fuck

There's-Always a Dumb-Bastard
That-Runs-His – Punk-Ass-Mouth
And-After – I-Beat-Him-Down
I-Feel-Like – I-Could-Use a Fuck
So-Here's – My-Song

(Chorus)
I Like To Fight And Fuck
I'll Whip Your Punk Ass
Then I'll Find A Woman To Fuck
I Like To Fight And Fuck
I'll Whip Your Punk Ass
Then I Might Even Fuck Your Woman
If She's Fuckable – That is

Wood Job (69.) (B.)

I-Have-The-Greatest – Lady
Anytime-I'm in The-Mood
She-Smiles & Says
Pull-Out-Your – Wood
And-I'll-Give-It a Job

My-Wood-Job-Lady is Perfect
I-Make-Love to Her
All-The-Time – Morning-Noon or Night
But-When-I – Come-Home-Sloshed
She-Smiles & Says – Pull-Out-Your
Wood & I'll-Give-It a Job

(Chorus)
Oh My Special Wood Job Lady
I Love You So Much
Oh My Special Wood Job Lady
I'm so Lucky I Met You
Oh My Special Wood Job Lady
I Hope You Never Get Tired Of
Giving Me Wood Job
My Heart Would Just Break In Two

I-Have-The-Greatest – Lady
Anytime-I'm in The-Mood
She-Smiles & Says
Pull-Out-Your – Wood
And-I'll-Give-It a Job

My-Wood-Job-Lady is Perfect
I-Make-Love to Her
All-The-Time – Morning-Noon or Night
But-When-I – Come-Home-Sloshed
She-Smiles & Says – Pull-Out-Your
Wood & I'll-Give-It a Job

(Chorus)

It's My 120th Song So Fuck You (120.) (B.)

You-Don't – Like-Me
Go-Fuck – Yourself
I'm-Tired of Being-Tired
Having to Prove-Myself
To-The-Jealous – To-The Flawed

I-Did-This – All on My-Own
I-Thank-No-One – Besides-Myself
If-I-Was-Like-You – I'd-Be-Stuck on #1
Not-On to #120
If-I-Was-Like-You – I'd-Be-Bored
While-Waiting on My-Time to Die

(Chorus)
It's My 120th Song
I've Decided To Add Some Fuck To It
So Fuck You If You Don't Like It
It's My 120th Song
I've Decided To Add Some Fuck To It
I'm Going To Be Me
And I Could Care Fucking Less
If You Fucking Like It Or Not

Being-Humble is For-The-Weak
I'll-Tell-You to Kiss-My-Ass
And-How to Fucking – Kiss-It
If-You-Don't – Like-That
Then-You-Can – Suck-on My-Shit

While-I-Party – While-I-Get-High
While-I-Get-Laid – Everyday of The Week
While-I – Live-My-Life
Any-Fucking-Way – I-Want-To
So-Remember – Fuck-You
If-You-Don't-Like-Me or My-Mind-Rockin'

(Repeat Chorus)